SECRETS 2

SECRETS 2

Not Perfect but Forgiven

Alicia Fleming

Paperback ISBN 978-0-9982270-3-0

Ebook ISBN 978-0-9982270-1-6

Printed in the United States of America

Cover design: Derrick Donelson

Cover photographs: Amy Conner Photography

ACKNOWLEDGEMENT

I would like to thank God again for allowing me the creativity, time, and energy to work full-time and continue writing. I have been so blessed this past year by the love of family and friends who have supported my dream to become a published author. This is my second book and I'm just as excited about this book as I was with the release of the first one. I ask God to make me an instrument to show His love, grace, and mercy to all that are imperfect but made perfect by His son – Jesus Christ. Some people are gifted to gab, preach, teach, and sing but my gift is writing. Now in my fifties, I am just now pursuing my dream. I continue to pray that one day soon, I will be able to read, write and travel full-time.

I can truly tell you that God put people in my path to help me throughout the process of getting my books published. I am forever grateful for every person. He continues to place people in my life that promote my book and share with others. A big thank you to my former pastor and mentor Pastor Woodrow W. Harris, Sr., and his wife Linda Harris for all their years of support and friendship and for teaching me through God's word how to walk through difficult times. I can't forget my sister and brother in the ministry, my big sister Pastor Terri Hunt, Memphis, Tennessee and friend and Pastor Fitzgerald Gilbert, Nashville, Tennessee. They have been walking ads for my book and I am forever grateful to them. Both should handle my PR and Marketing for me – LOL! Last but not least, my ride or die girls/sister/ girlfriends who continue to share my books with others, Philippia Bellefant, Renee Martin, Jerrica Harlan, Gloria Holland. Thanks for my book cover designer, Derrick Donelson who always delivers what I'm looking for in my book covers. He has also designed a beautiful logo for my brand. I am forever grateful to Cheryl Mason who edits my books along with Tyora Moody who does my book trailers and formatting for me. I give her my ideas and she runs with it and delivers an amazing book trailer for me. I would also like to thank the women of the Christian Book Lovers Retreat who poured into me mightily last year and encouraged me on this journey especially Valarie Lewis Coleman and Rochinda Pickens as well as those ladies at the retreat who purchased my book. Vanessa Miller and Tyora Moody, thanks for the new writing opportunities you have given me – all you ladies are so amazing.

I continue to thank my husband, David, for all his love, support and encouragement, my daughter, Megan along with my Dad, Andrew Clemmons, Sr. and my brother, Drew and sister Lynette who always support me in whatever I'm doing. I am forever grateful for this gift and I pray that He expands it to the New York Times Best Seller's List and even a movie – yes, I dream big. We have not because we ask not. I continue to stand on the promise of Jeremiah 29:11.

Continue to walk in God's blessings
Alicia

SANIYA & ISLAND

A New Season

As service was being dismissed at 12:30 on Sunday, Saniya thought about the last year and a half and how much her life had changed. She had gone off to college, fallen in love, had her heart broken by Xavier and then decided to take a hiatus from dating. It was hard to believe that she had completed her first two years of college and was now a junior.

She thought about Jason and her short-term relationship with him. She had met Jason at a party that Dee and her friends had dragged her out to one night. They hit it off and started dating. She and Jason had a blast together talking, listening to music and discussing their future career plans. When they got out for break that semester, she and Jason talked on the phone and he had come to meet her parents and she had even taken him to meet her grandparents one day. She hadn't met anyone in his family yet but was looking forward to meeting them. About a month prior to the semester beginning, Saniya hadn't heard from Jason. He told her he was not returning the next semester but was going to take a break. Saniya wasn't sure what that meant until she returned to the campus. When she returned to campus, she found out that Jason had gotten married. It appears that he had been living a double life and had another girlfriend back home that he had been dating while he was also seeing her. His girlfriend had gotten pregnant and Jason married her but didn't have the decency to let her know about any of this; Saniya had to find out from the gossip on campus. She felt like a fool when she learned what had happened, so she had decided to forget about men and concentrate totally on her school work. On top of the news about Jason, Xavier had started calling to check on her. She didn't want to get excited about him calling and now their phone calls were just awkward since they were no longer a couple. He would always apologize for everything and she would end up crying, so she decided to no longer take his calls. Deep in her heart, she knew she still loved Xavier, but she was not going to let him hurt her again.

"God, I don't know if you are listening to me or not but there are times that I feel like I am such a failure in the relationship department. Every time that I think I have met a good, Christian guy, they end up hurting me and I just don't understand what I am doing wrong. I am not the one seeking out these guys, but they end up approaching me and initiating the relationship. You said in Proverbs 18:22, 'He who finds a wife finds what is good and receives favor from the Lord.' I thought all the decent guys were at church, but it seems like I should just forget that idea and maybe find me someone at the club or in the streets because the guys from church are letdowns as well. Will I ever find true love and someone that doesn't hurt me? When I love, I love hard and maybe the problem is that I always try and see the good in people, but they are bad guys. I don't know what else to do anymore other than just give up on the whole dating thing. I am going to focus on school and nothing else at this time."

Simultaneously, at 12:30 as service was being dismissed, Island sat and thought about how much his life had changed in the past year or so. He was no longer bar hopping and getting drunk, no longer having one-night stands and was staying strictly in the word of God. The only thing that Island did was work and go to church service. He had thrown himself full force into studying the word and reviewing music and songs for the choir. Sometimes, he would even go out to eat with some of the choir members just to get out of the house. He had also stopped cruising the parks and hanging out because that always led to temptation and Island was trying to get his life back together.

"I will concentrate on trying to be a good big brother to Saniya so that I can try and keep these vipers out of her life." Saniya had shared at the tribe meeting how she had met a nice guy at college and started dating him but again she ended up with a broken heart. Island hoped that he could shed some insight from a man's point of view to Saniya and hope that the next time she met someone, she would be better equipped. He was now going to hang out with his little sister for the rest of the day.

In the parking lot, Saniya heard someone call out her name.

"Hey Saniya, how are you? It's good to see you," Island said smiling at Saniya while giving her a big old bear hug.

"I'm great Island, how are you?"

"I can't complain. I feel like we haven't had a chance to sit down and talk in a long time, why don't we grab some lunch; that is without our Mothers?"

"Okay, let's do it, that sounds like a plan," Saniya said.

"Why don't you drop your car off at home and I will swing by in about 15 minutes and pick you up?"

"Okay, that's cool."

"See ya then."

Saniya thought it would be fun catching up with Island since they hadn't hung out in some time.

Island thought it would be great fun as well just like old times; he missed talking to her. She was the little sister that he never had in his life. He hated that Xavier had broken her heart but at least he could stay close by and be a listening ear and a big brother for her. Saniya was a beautiful young lady and Island thought at one point and time years ago that he and Saniya could have had a dating relationship but once he realized that Saniya wasn't interested in him, he decided to cancel out that idea in his mind. Not to mention, he had another issue that had stopped him in his past and he didn't trust anybody enough to tell them what happened. Other than Taylor, Saniya was the only other woman that Island had even thought about being in a relationship with where he could learn to be happy and have a good time with a woman. Island thought, "there are just some things that you should keep to yourself but look at the mess that has caused in my life."

Island pulled up at Saniya's house and rang the doorbell. "Hello Island, come on in," Saniya's mother exclaimed.

"I haven't seen you in sometime, how's your Mama doing?"

"She's doing fine and probably trying to figure out why I haven't showed up at her house for dinner today," he laughed.

"So, you and Saniya are dodging your Mamas today? You know we are both going to get you and Saniya back for excluding us?"

"I know the two of you will not let us forget this, now will you?" Island said and kissed Saniya's mom on the cheek.

"Saniya, Island is here."

"Tell him, I will be right down."

Island had been trying to consume himself with work and hanging out with his tribe from church to keep his mind off his personal issues. He was still wrestling with some familiar feelings and staying away from his old habits. He thought maybe he would be able to share some with Saniya but wasn't sure if she was ready for all his drama.

"Girl, come on, I'm hungry! You are not on a date with a knucklehead, it's just me!" Island yelled.

"Oh, you got jokes?" Saniya yelled from upstairs. She was laughing as she came down the stairs.

"I'm ready, are you happy now?"

"I will be once I can eat and relax," Island said.

"Mama, we're gone."

"Okay, ya'll have a good time and Island don't forget to tell your Mama I said hello."

"Yes ma'am, I will." Saniya and Island then headed out the door for an afternoon of fun and catching up.

"Where are we going to eat at Island? I am starving like Marvin."

"Okay, Hungry Hippo what do you have a taste for? Do you think you can hold out until we get downtown or do I need to find something closer to home?" Island said, teasing Saniya.

"For you to be so small, you have a doggone appetite like one of the brothas," Island said.

"Really Island? Hungry Hippo and now I have an appetite like one of the bros?" Saniya slapped him on the arm.

"Ouch girl, you hit like one of the bros as well."

"Whatever," Saniya said laughing.

"Do you think you could make it to Fifth Quarter – the steakhouse over off Murfreesboro Road? You know I love their prime rib and their lobster bites are to die for."

"Yes, they are! My boyfriend in high school took me there for prom one year and it is good. But Island, that cost too much, you know I'm a college student on a budget," Saniya exclaimed.

"Did I say anything about you paying chicken head?"

Saniya rolled her eyes at Island and said, "No, you didn't, but I don't want to get there and have to do dishes either. I am not going to be too many more hungry hippos and chicken heads – boy you better watch yourself before you get checked!" Island almost wrecked his car laughing at her.

"It's my treat and the least I can do since we haven't hung out in a while and after all I am the one with the full-time job."

They arrived at Fifth Quarter and got a table and started looking at the menu. Saniya thought to herself, "I wish I could find a guy just like Island, someone that I could have fun with and also someone who has their life together."

"Saniya, what are you over there thinking about?"

"I was just thinking that I wished I could find a guy just like you Island, someone who has their head on straight and has their life together."

"That is flattering Saniya and thanks for the compliment, but I should tell you that I don't have all my stuff together. I may look like I have it together, but I am still struggling with some things but of course you know that because of our prayer group. Everything that is wrapped up in a pretty package, isn't always what it's cracked up to be. Nobody is perfect Saniya and you must stop looking for perfection. Are you perfect?"

"Well, no I'm not" Saniya responded with a puzzled look.

"Saniya, you are a beautiful young lady and God has someone very special out there for you, but you have to let God put you together."

"I know Island, but I have always wanted to be married and have a family and it's not like I'm out at the clubs or in the streets looking for these guys, they end up approaching me. Maybe I am sending out the wrong vibes. I try and carry myself in a lady-like manner, I'm professional at work and I don't run around half naked or cursing or carousing so why can't I find a good guy?"

"Well for one, you shouldn't be looking for a good guy. The Bible says that *'He who finds a wife, finds a good thing.'* *(Proverbs 18:22)* Saniya, know what the Bible says about you and who you are in Christ and all the rest will fall into place for you. At the end of the day, we all want the same thing – someone to love and someone to love us back unconditionally accepting the good and the bad in us."

Island could see Saniya's eyes start to well up with tears and he grabbed her hand and said, "I'm always here for you Saniya and if you want me to check out any of these knuckleheads that want to date you, I don't mind doing so. I will bust them up if they mess over my little sister – you know I don't play when it comes to you. It took everything in me not to bust Xavier in the head when he hurt you."

"Thanks Island, I really appreciate that. You are so sweet, and I may take you up on this 'screening process,' as they both laughed.

"What about you?" Saniya asked.

"Well, I'm still staying on the straight and narrow," Island said, half laughing. "It is still a struggle for me because I still have thoughts about guys, but I have been doing good. I'm still going to counseling and still meeting up with Deacon Jones and Pastor Harris to talk through some things, so I'm getting there. Of course, I have kept myself from temptation and away from some of my old friends because I don't feel that I am strong enough to be in certain company just yet. I just ask that you keep praying for me Saniya, it's hard out here in the real world and trying to meet someone who will accept you for who you are."

Saniya had hoped that Island had met a nice female but now realized that Island was still struggling with his sexuality. She continued praying for him. She wanted him to be happy and to have someone to share his life with. They both wanted the same thing, but both apparently were looking for love in all the wrong places. They laughed and reminisced until they looked at the time and saw that it was around 6:00 and they had been there since 2:00.

"My how time flies when you're having fun," Island said.

"Girl let's get out of here. I have work tomorrow and I'm sure you have other things to do as well in getting ready for the week." Saniya laughed and agreed and the two of them jumped back in Island's beamer and headed back home for the night.

As they were driving back home, Island said, "Saniya, I meant it when I told you that I would check out any prospects. I really don't want to see you hurt again. You made me want to whoop Xavier's a—" he caught himself. "I about lost my religion when he broke your heart. I was ready to get him for hurting you."

"Boy you are crazy, I have to accept my role in that relationship as well. I was trying to be a big girl and be grown and move too fast. I must confess to you that I still think about him and I still love him and probably always will. He was my first" and she stopped.

"I know, you don't have to tell me, we have all been there but trust me when I tell you that God is going to send you

Mr. Right, just hold on and be patient. You want a man that will be able to love you as Christ loved the church. One thing that often happens with young women is that they leave their Daddy's house and go right into another man's house and they don't find out who they really are and what they want out of life. I call it the Cinderella complex – waiting on Prince Charming to come and sweep you off your feet and live happily ever after. Relationships are hard work, so I can only imagine marriage has got to be even more difficult. You have two different people coming together trying to be one with different mindsets and backgrounds and you are trying to make it work. You must do what works for you in your relationship and forget about the fairytale. What happens after the honeymoon is over? The electric company or the gas company don't take love payments, they want some money." Island could tell that Saniya was listening intently to him and thinking about all that he was saying. He was praying that he was saying the right things; things that would make her stop and think. He needed to take some of his own advice. As they pulled up to Saniya's house, Island said, "Love you Niya," and gave her a hug.

"Love you too Island" Saniya responded as she jumped out the car and closed the door.

"Have a great week and thanks for lunch and our talks – that stay between us – don't tell our Mamas what we talked about." They both laughed.

ISLAND

Pressing toward the Mark

After Island dropped Saniya off at home, he had some time to reflect upon their conversation and his own life over the last year. He was still trying to adjust to the new lifestyle he had committed himself to since joining the prayer group. He was studying the Bible more than he ever had in his entire life. He had cut off several friends and he had stopped the bar scene and picking up guys. He even stopped going to the park on Sunday afternoons. He felt like he had become an old man over the last year or so because it seemed like the only thing he did was go to work, home and to church and then start all over again.

"My life has become so dull," Island said to himself.

"It is so routine now, no excitement at all." Island knew deep down that he needed this time alone if nothing more than to give his body a break from the late-night hours, alcohol and sex. He had started going to the gym a lot more especially since he wasn't having any extracurricular activity which helped with his stress level. He needed to sit down and have a heart to heart with Deacon Jones to see how he handled being single again and not having someone to be intimate with on these lonely nights.

"Lord, it's hard following you on the straight and narrow," Island said out loud.

"What's a man to do when he isn't married and wants to have someone special in their life to share their dreams with?" Of course, Island still hadn't made up his mind one hundred percent about being in a relationship with a woman and how he would even start a conversation with a woman about his past and his feelings. Feelings that he was still unsure about even today. He was trying hard to change his life around, but some days were better than others.

"I am really trying Lord, but I am struggling with all of this. I want to follow what your word says but what do I do about my feelings that I have for another man? It should be okay for me to love who I want to love but your word says that you would hold that against me." Island knew that he was just trying to justify his behavior and what he wanted to do.

"I guess I should get back in this word and study some more so that I can stop questioning you about what I want to do." Island decided to listen to some praise music so that he could pick out some new selections for the choir, so he put on his earphones and began listening. As he was listening to his music, he didn't realize that his phone was ringing, and Cameron's name was on the display.

In the spiritual realm, the enemy was willing Island to pick up the phone, but that distraction didn't work. Island was in the middle of listening to his praise music. The enemy murmured to himself, I will keep throwing distractions at him because I know his weakness and that just makes my job even easier. I will give him what he likes, and I know exactly how to package it, laughing to himself.

LOLITA

A New Attitude

As Lolita thought about how crazy and insane her life had been recently, she couldn't help but be thankful and grateful that she was starting a new chapter of her life. Initially, it was all very scary, and she didn't know how she was going to make it without Rashad but then she remembered that she had once been an independent woman prior to Rashad and her daughter. She remembered that she had a life and promising career. She thought about how she had made Rashad and her daughter the center of her universe and forgot about her dreams and aspirations. Her marriage with Rashad had been over for some time. She was just now having the courage to do what she needed to do. Although, she had grounds to divorce Rashad biblically, it still hurt. She also knew that this was an opportunity for forgiveness and restoration, so she had decided to forgive Rashad and to move on. She knew that God hated divorce, but she felt justified because of the circumstances. She had known for some time that Rashad had been unfaithful, but she didn't want to rock the boat because she wanted to keep the lifestyle that she had grown accustomed to. She just looked the other way and let Rashad do what he wanted, and she continued to live the luxurious lifestyle that she had always wanted. She did love and care about Rashad but had to come to realize that her entire relationship had started off as a lie. She should not have gotten married just because she was pregnant.

She had seen it many times in her life when a young lady got pregnant out of wedlock and the parents made them get married. Inevitably, it ended up in divorce somewhere down the road. Although Big Mama didn't know she was pregnant, she and Rashad had decided to elope and get married and now she realized he was only doing so to be honorable. Deep down, he wasn't over Shelby. So, the entire relationship was like trying to put a square peg into a round hole; trying to force the situation and make it work. She remembered one night when they had been intimate, he yelled out Shelby's name and not her name. It was like someone had stabbed her in the heart, but she continued moving forward with him in their relationship. She hadn't considered that Shelby may have still loved him, and she had to realize that she herself was jealous of her own sister and had wanted Rashad for herself. She had been tired of Shelby always getting all the guys' attention and when she and Rashad started hanging out and there was some chemistry there, she didn't stop it. She should have, but she became selfish and was more like her sister than she was willing to admit.

"Now, it's my turn. My turn to do what makes me happy and to find out who I really am. I have been walking in

Shelby's shadow all these years trying to be something that I'm not and now I need to trust and believe God for the man that He has for me. Maybe this new bible study that I have started will get me on the right track, as well as me joining the singles ministry at church. All this counseling and all these emotions that I have been going through has been painful but at the same time, cleansing for me. Now, it's time for my restoration and healing and I am ready to keep it moving. I don't know if my relationship with my sister will ever be the same, but I can't hate her or resent her for everything that has happened because I played a big part in it as well."

About that time, Pastor Harris was saying the benediction and Lolita said, "Amen" and service was dismissed. As she headed to her car, a gentleman that she hadn't seen before said hello to her. She smiled and said hello back.

"Hmmmmm, who is that tall, dark drink of water?" Lolita said to herself.

"I am going to keep it moving because everything that looks good to you, ain't good for you," she said to herself. Her marriage had been a prime example of that old saying. On the outside, she and Rashad appeared to be the perfect couple but that was so far from the truth and the reality of their situation.

"I have got to focus on my new career and the new me." Lolita had always wanted to own her own boutique with clothes, shoes and accessories and she had found the perfect location in Greenhills for her new place. With the settlement she received in the divorce from Rashad, along with her alimony, she could now pursue her dream and make her own money. Things were beginning to look up for her. Their daughter was adjusting and so was she. She still had to see Rashad when he came over to pick up their daughter, but each time it got easier. They had begun to be cordial to one another and learned to stop making snide comments to one another. She would do anything for the sake of her daughter and that included being cordial to Rashad. He was hurt because of the pain he had caused his daughter and he regretted her being caught in the middle of this mess. He and Lolita talked with her about everything in hopes she would understand that none of this was her fault. They also had her in counseling because they wanted to ensure that she adjusted to everything and understood that she didn't do anything to cause the turmoil that had taken place in their lives recently.

"I am embracing this new beginning in my life and I can't wait to see what God has in store for me." Lolita had come to realize that God only wanted the best for her. She had learned a lot about herself over the last year or so and she was excited about finding herself and discovering her passion again. It was like she was receiving a second chance at life.

"This is what my life should have been like all this time without the stress and distrust of my husband." Lolita started enjoying being alone with herself and having her time alone with God. She had started going to the gym to work out when she had the time and she was also spending more time with her daughter doing fun things now that she was older.

She had a peace about herself that she had never known could exist and now she hated that she had wasted so much time being miserable.

"It is so true, 'I can do bad all by myself, I don't need any extra help.'"

SHELBY

Reminiscing

As Shelby bowed her head during alter call, she thought about everything that had taken place recently and thanked God that she still had her sanity. She had asked God to forgive her for all the pain that she had caused James along with Lolita. She knew that she was walking on egg shells with James and things were very different between them right now. She felt like a prisoner in her own marriage now but had felt some freedom when everyone found out about her and Rashad. It had been crazy but liberating at the same time. She just didn't know that James was going to hold her hostage in the marriage. She did love James and they had a beautiful life together, but she was still in love with Rashad and didn't know what to do about it. Rashad had been calling and they had chatted some on the phone, but she hadn't made up her mind on what she was going to do. Maybe she could convince James that they could co-parent and move on with their lives like Lolita and Rashad were doing but she thought he would never go for it.

"I just can't lose my children" she told Rashad. He understood. Then again, he didn't.

"Maybe the two of us can sit down and talk to James calmly," Rashad said to Shelby.

"No, I don't think that is such a good idea right now. James is like a prison guard checking in on me and being mean to me. It is a very awkward situation right now and I don't want you to get in the middle of this mess. James is still very angry and I'm afraid of what he might say or do if you approach him."

Rashad had reminded Shelby that he was part of the mess that had been created. He was willing to do whatever it took to be with her but at the same time, he was hurt that she didn't just make the decision and go for it and be with him. They had wanted to be together all this time over so many years and now that they had the opportunity to do so, she was scared.

"Maybe I can keep James at bay long enough until I figure out what to do. I do still love Rashad and I care about James and the life we have built. How do you love two people at the same time? I love James, but I am *in love* with Rashad. What am I going to do? Rashad has had my heart for so many years.... I just can't bear the thought of not having him in my life at all."

Even though they had been apart for some years, Shelby was always able to talk to Rashad and see him at family functions. She was afraid that if she didn't take this chance with Rashad now that she would lose him forever.

"Still, I need to know what to do with my relationship with James and how my children will be affected regardless of the decision that I make. I don't know what to do for my sake or my children."

"Do I stay in a marriage that isn't really loving or do I move on with Rashad and let my children adapt to their new life with Rashad and me? This is like a Lifetime movie for sure with no clear resolution. Either way someone will get hurt."

"Amen," the crowd said, and Shelby raised her head to see that everyone was going back to their seats from alter call.

Shelby said her goodbyes to everyone and decided to stop by Big Mama's house on her way home to chat with her. Her grandmother still drove herself to church on Sundays and then back home to fix Sunday dinner. For a while, Shelby hadn't stopped by Big Mama's house as much because she didn't want to get a lecture. But she had decided that she needed to let go and listen to her grandmother. After all, Big Mama didn't get to be her age being stupid. She always had a nugget of wisdom to share with her and Lolita.

"Big Mama, where you at?" Shelby yelled when she didn't see her upon entering the house.

"I'm right here chile" Big Mama was coming in from the garage.

"Big Mama, I know that you are not just getting home from church, are you?"

"You mind where your feet take you to and I will mind where mine take me. You just make sure that your feet are taking you in the right direction that you need to go. They have taken you in the wrong direction for some time and look where that got you."

"I know Big Mama, they got me in a lot of trouble."

"Yes, they did, and you and your sister are at least speaking to one another and being half way decent and I don't want to see that change. You two are all you got if anything ever happens to me, so you need to learn how to love one another and coexist with one another." Shelby knew that her grandmother was telling the truth, so she just responded and said, "yes ma'am."

"By the way what is going on with you and James now days?"

"Nothing. I still feel like a prisoner in my own house and Rashad keeps pressuring me to make a decision."

"Well why haven't you run to Rashad? You couldn't wait to be with him when he was with your sister and now you all hesitant about being with him. Isn't that what you wanted all of these years?"

"I thought so too, Big Mama, but not at the expense of my children."

"Chile, that man ain't going to take your children from you. He is just blowing smoke. Any time that you have to make someone a prisoner in a relationship and not trust them, they are just doing it to make you miserable. Deep down James knows that you are a good mother. He is just hurt by all of this. I believe that if you continue praying and asking God to help you that He will move on James' heart and soften it to the point where you two can sit down like adults and move on with or without each other. Nothing is impossible with God, Shelby. Nothing."

Shelby sat and thought about what her grandmother was

saying, and she realized she should have had a heart to heart with her years ago and maybe her life would have been different. Maybe if she and Lolita had worked out their issues of abandonment by their mother, their lives would have turned out differently and they wouldn't have spent so much time hurting one another.

Big Mama never talked about their mama and therefore they didn't bring her up either. They just knew that something bad had happened and the relationship between their mother and Big Mama had come to a screeching halt and they ended up living with Big Mama. Shelby remembers the day that their mother left and never came back. She and Big Mama had a huge fight and their mother stormed out of the house yelling, "You do what you want to, I don't want them anyway. I have my life to live." They never heard from their mother again nor saw her. They would ask Big Mama every now and then about their mother and her eyes would tear up and she would just say. "One day Jesus will bring her back home just like the prodigal son." So far that day hadn't come. Shelby and Lolita learned to live life without their mother, but it never stopped them from thinking about her and what happened to her or why she wanted to leave them or why she didn't take them with her; they had so many unanswered questions.

"Big Mama, I don't want you to get mad at me, but you have been talking to Lolita and me about love and forgiveness most of our lives. It brings up questions within me about you and our Mama. Do you still love her, and have you forgiven her for leaving the way she did?"

Big Mama paused for a moment and said, "Yes, I still love her because she's my child and yes I forgave her a long time ago, but I haven't forgotten the hell she put me through – some things you never forget. Plus, I had the joy of raising my two granddaughters and seeing them become beautiful young ladies. Yes, it was hard raising you girls after she left but I did the best with the situation that I was handed. Did I make the right decisions all the time? No, but I did the best I could. Could I have reached out to her years ago? Yes, I could have, but she made her choices and I made mine and life goes on regardless of how painful it is."

"I'm sorry Big Mama," Shelby said.

"No, don't be sorry chile. The Lord said that we would have trials and tribulations and you never know what they will be, and you can only control how you respond to the situations; nothing else."

Shelby kissed her grandmother and told her she loved her and then left to go home. When she left, Big Mama was sitting in her rocking chair on the front porch humming her favorite hymn. Shelby then wished that she hadn't said what she did because it appeared to have put her grandmother in a somber mood. Part of Shelby wished that her mother would come back to see them but then there was part of her that wanted to keep her heart shut up from more pain — and she especially didn't want to cause her grandmother any more pain now that she was up in her latter years.

DEACON JONES

A Little Pep in My Step

As Deacon Jones was listening to Pastor Harris wrap up his sermon, he reminisced about the past year or so about all that had happened to him. He had gone from being a "fake Christian" to becoming a real disciple and follower of Jesus Christ. He thought about how distorted his perception of Christianity had been all these years. He had thought that coming to church, reading his Bible and dressing up on Sunday's was all he needed to do to be a Christian. Boy, had he been wrong but the sad thing about it was that there were a lot of people that had the same perception that he had. He never really understood how much God loved him, even during all his wrongdoings. How He had sacrificed His son's life so that he could have the life he now led. He still had days where he missed Mona and wished so desperately that she could see him now. He had made up his mind to be real after his Damascus road experience with the Lord, like Saul/Paul. His experience was so painful that he knew deep in his heart that things had to change. He was angry with the Lord for a short time until he realized he was the one that was to blame for the way things turned out, not the Lord.

The Lord allows things to happen that we will never be able to understand. He says in His word, '*My thoughts are not your thoughts and my ways are not your ways*' – *Isaiah 55:8-9*.

When Pastor Harris yelled, "Amen church" that's when Deacon Jones snapped out of his thoughts. As he looked around and saw Sister Lula, he smiled and was reminded that he had learned to be happy again; something he never thought would happen.

"Hey Deacon, how are things going?"

"They're going just fine Pastor," Deacon Jones responded. "If I was any better, I couldn't stand myself," he said laughing.

"That's great to hear Deacon. What have you and this young lady been up to lately?" Pastor Harris smiled at Sister Lula.

"Oh, nothing much," Deacon Jones could see that Sister Lula was blushing. She was a beautiful woman even in her seasoned years, so Deacon knew that she had to have been absolutely stunning in her younger years. It hadn't mattered to him that she was older than him, he had been in awe at her grace and beauty. She was truly a woman of God and she had reminded him a lot of Mona, but just an older version.

"We are about to head out and grab some lunch and then start getting ready for our tribe meeting on next week. We are still holding the monthly meetings and our little group has bonded so well that everyone shares now, and we are able to pray for one another and give scriptural responses; not just our personal responses. Our tribe meeting has accomplished the task of being a no judgement zone and it has become a great refuge for our group to share with one another. We also get out in the community feeding the hungry and clothing the homeless as we are instructed according to Matthew 25:36."

"I am so proud of you all Deacon, it makes my heart glad to see this come to fruition. You see, it starts small and continues to bloom and grow. Just like a plant, you plant the seed, water it, fertilize it and watch it grow. We all play a small part."

"We wouldn't have been able to do it without your direction Pastor. You have been very encouraging to each one of us in the group and we truly appreciate you."

"Just keep doing what you are doing Deacon and you too Sister Lula. We need more seasoned saints like you to help teach these young folks what this Christian journey is all about. It's a hard road for us at times but if we want to reign with Christ then there are times that we must suffer with him as well."

"So true Pastor and I didn't understand that until this past year. I have had people lie on me, laugh at me and just plain be mean to me after all that took place the last year. I have had to hold my head high and keep pressing toward the mark which is in Christ Jesus."

"Pastor, we have some new ideas that we want to run by you for this upcoming year so please let us know when you are available for us to meet with you," Sister Lula said.

"Just call my office Sister Lula and the secretary will slot some time on my calendar for me to meet with you and

Deacon Jones. I can't wait to hear what you two young people have come up with." They all laughed.

SANIYA

New Beginnings

Saniya found it hard to believe how fast her life was moving and it was moving along without a man. She and Dee were no longer roommates but still very close friends. Since she had pledged her sorority, she had started sharing an apartment with one of her sorority sisters named Sierra. They were thick as glue and did a lot of stuff together. Dee had pledged another sorority, but they were still sisters regardless of the colors and Greek letters that they were sporting. She and Sierra partied together, cooked together and had a love for good food. They had a blast as roommates because they were so similar. They both had lost their virginity to their first love although Sierra was still with her boyfriend. Saniya had moved on without Xavier. She thought about him a lot lately.

"Sierra, this is the time that I should be planning my graduation along with my marriage. After all, that's one reason our parents send us off to these fancy colleges so that we can get a good education and meet a husband. Our Mothers taught us to go to school, get a career not just a job, get married and then start a family. No one told us what to do if things didn't go in this order. No one told us that we would have to kiss a few frogs before we met Prince Charming. No one told us that we would have our hearts broken and become a basket case when you can't be with the one you love. Who prepares us for life? We see all these movies where everyone lives happily ever after but what about how to handle from once upon a time until you get to happily ever after. No one taught us how to handle all the bad stuff you go through to get to happily ever after. Is there such a thing?"

"Girl, you are going too deep for me right now. I can't answer any of those questions any more than you can. I truly believe that Xavier loved you and cared about you, but he was scared. You never know, Saniya, the two of you could end up back together. Right now, I wish you were back with him cause you are making my head hurt." Sierra then threw a pillow at her across the room and started laughing.

"No, Sierra, I am moving forward not backwards."

"Okay, I hear you," Sierra said.

Later that day as Saniya arrived at work, she caught a glimpse of this guy out the corner of her eye. He smiled and came over to her.

"Hi, I'm Micah, and you are?"

"Hi, I'm Saniya."

"Saniya?" "What a beautiful name. I don't think I've seen you around here before," Micah said.

"That's because I am away at school and I am just home

for the long holiday weekend. When I'm home during the holidays and summer, I work here at the store."

"Well, it was nice meeting you Saniya and I hope to see ya around."

"Okay, sure" Saniya said awkwardly.

Brandy ran over and said, "Girl, he is only the finest brotha up in this store. Every girl in here has been trying to get his attention and he comes right over to you college girl." Micah was a fair-skinned brotha with gray eyes along with being tall and slender. He had an athletic build and was bow legged. He also had an accent like he was from the north; no Southern drawl. Saniya was trying not to drool – she knew the brotha was fine, but she was trying to play it cool.

"Girl, I'm not paying any attention to him, although he is cute."

"Cute? Girl, he is straight up fine. You may need to get your eyes checked if you are just seeing cute," Brandy said twisting her hair around her finger and smacking her gum.

"No, I'm just focusing on trying to get out of college and get my career and life started. I don't have time to play games with these crazy guys out here. I had my heart broken not long ago and I don't care to get back on that merry go round again anytime soon."

"Well, I understand that, so I will see you on lunch break. Saniya went back to working.

Later that day, Saniya went to the break room to rest for a few minutes and Micah was there finishing up his break. He was reading a book when she came in the break room.

"Saniya, have you been having a good day?"

"Yes, it's been busy, but I like it like that – it makes the day go by faster than just sitting around."

"What do you do for fun? I mean when you're not in school."

"Not a whole lot anymore. I am just trying to concentrate on finishing up school and I also have an upcoming internship to do my last year, so it doesn't leave too much time for a social life. By the time I get home for summer and the holidays and see a few family and friends and try and hang out for a little bit, the break is over."

"A group of my friends and I are going to the movies tomorrow night if you would like to join me, I mean us? I promise, it will be good clean fun. We won't stay out late because I have to be at church on Sunday morning to usher."

Saniya was caught off guard by the question but said, "Oh, okay, how about I let you know for sure on tomorrow."

When Saniya got home she told her Mom about the guy at work and that he had asked her out to the movies, her mother caught her off guard for the second time in one day and said, "Why don't you go?"

"I don't know Mama. I just met the guy and all the girls are smiling and grinning at him and he seems nice enough but" ...."

"Oh Saniya, stop it! You need to move on past Xavier and start going back out having fun. All you do is go to school and work and that's not healthy. I didn't say go and fall in love with the guy but try and get out of the house some. You have to have some balance, you will be out working full-time soon enough. And what happened to Jason? I thought you were seeing him, or has that already fizzled out?"

Saniya just didn't have the heart to tell her mom what she had learned about Jason, so she just told her that she moved on and so did Jason. The sad thing is that her family had met Jason and loved him.

"That would be my luck, the guy that everyone loves cheats and the one that everyone hates, cheats." Saniya decided to take a chance and called back to the store to see if Micah was still at work and he was.

"Hello, Micah, this is Saniya."

"Hey there. How are you?"

"I'm good, she said.

"Is everything okay?" Micah asked.

"Yes, I didn't have your number and found out that I'm off tomorrow, but I did want to let you know that I would like to hang out with you and your friends and go to the movies."

"Oh, that's great. I'm glad you decided to take me up on my offer. I was hoping that I would have seen you before you left the store today, but I got busy and that didn't happen so I'm glad that you called. Can I get your number so that I can call you later tonight, so we can chat some more?"

"Sure" and Saniya gave Micah her number. Saniya thought to herself, "We will see what happens from here but I'm not expecting too much."

Later that night Micah called Saniya and they talked for about an hour or so, finding out more about one another. Saniya found out that Micah was the oldest of three children like she was. He was also working at the store part-time because he was just finishing up with college and was looking for a job in his field of engineering. He was in a fraternity and was graduating at the top of his class in the spring. He loved sports and had played basketball in high school but not at their university. He came from a two-parent home and both of his parents were college graduates. He was looking to relocate to California or even New York. He said he would go wherever he could get a foot in the door to jump start his career. He was like Saniya in that he wanted to live in a big metropolitan city and before Saniya knew it, they had talked for hours on the phone. "Maybe this will be an exciting year after all," she thought to herself, but she didn't want to get her hopes up too high.

ISLAND MAN

Temptation is just around the corner

As Island was finishing up his conference call, there was a knock on his office door.

"Come in."

"Island how are things going today?" his boss Mr. Jones asked.

"All is well, Mr. Jones, and yourself?"

"If I were any better, Island, I wouldn't be able to stand myself" he said laughing. "I would like to talk to you about something. I have a proposition for you. The firm is wanting to open an office in the Miami area and your name came up as one of the partners that we want to have go and stay in Miami for a few months to get things up and running. You are an asset to the firm, Island, and we have big plans for your career here. You have excelled beyond our goals and your team and fellow employees love you. You have the utmost respect from everyone here and we want to take you to the next level in this industry. We are also opening another location in New York City, but I thought you would prefer the Miami heat opposed to the cold of the Big Apple. But I will let you make the final determination. Both cities have a lot to offer a young man like yourself, but I think the Miami deal would be a better fit for your career."

"Wow, Mr. Jones, I appreciate the kind words and I appreciate the offer. What are the dates for the office opening up?"

"We want to have the office up and running by January 1 and with the summer ending soon and fall fast approaching, we wanted to give you enough time to hand off some of your files here and to get prepared for the office opening. You will have all the resources that you need, and we have a nice luxurious corporate apartment that is move-in ready with all the amenities that a bachelor like yourself could want. We know it will be hard work and a lot of hours, so we do what we can to make you very comfortable while you are working remotely and getting us up and running in a new city."

"So, I would need to leave for Miami in the next month or so?"

"Yes, we would like to have you there at least by September 1st to get the ball rolling. That gives you four months to get setup and get a staff in place and trained. We have all the confidence in the world that you are the man for this one, Island, and that you won't let us down. Miami will be our biggest up and coming office. We already have our eyes on people from this office that we would like to relocate that will make the office run smooth and expand some other careers. Give it some thought and get back to me by the end of the week."

"Would I have to stay in Miami?" Island asked.

"No, not necessarily. We can discuss that portion later. As I said, give it some thought and get back to me in a few days."

Island couldn't believe that his boss was giving him this opportunity but at the same time, he was excited about doing something new and proving to the rest of the partners that he was worthy of the position. He knew that Miami would be the office because of the strong suggestion from his boss but they wanted to make it look like New York was an option. Island had already lived in New York, and not to mention, Taylor was still there so he had already made it up in his mind that he didn't want to go back to New York. He still had mixed emotions about the city; both good and bad. Just when Island was having a good time with his church family and reconnecting with Saniya, now he would have to leave again, but at least it was only temporary.

"Man, I will miss everybody here, but it will also give me a chance to have a different scenery for a minute and maybe some of my friends can come visit me and get out of Nashville during the winter and head south to see me." He thought his family and friends would appreciate that offer but Island already knew he wouldn't have a lot of down time, but he would try and have some fun while he was there. After all, he would need some downtime. Island dreaded telling his Mama that he was going to be on the road again. She was always so emotional when it came to him and especially him leaving to go somewhere else and work. His Mama still would not get on a plane at her age. Island often joked with her about flying and one thing he didn't understand was how Christian folks are some of the scariest folks on the planet. He would often ask his Mama, how are you going to be telling me how great Jesus is and quote scripture but then be scared and worried about everything? He finally started quoting scriptures to her *from 2 Timothy 5:7 – God has not given us a spirit of fear but of power, love, and a sound mind* along with *I can do all things through Christ who strengthens me*. His Mama would laugh but then just say, "I'm not going up in the air, I will be in the air when I meet Jesus and not before then." Island had finally given up on convincing his Mama to experience new things. The fear factor had been woven into her DNA and she was scared of everything. Island finally said to his Mama, "You either have faith or fear but you can't have both at the same time." That had apparently gotten her attention and made her stop and think. He could tell the word was working on her and she was trying, but change is hard for people. We don't like to be made to be uncomfortable not realizing that God is a progressive God and He doesn't want us stagnant in any aspect of our lives. Island recalled his conversation with his Mama.

"We can't keep doing the same things repeatedly and expecting a different result. That is the definition of insanity."

She would roll her eyes and ignore him and then continue to operate in fear instead of stepping out on faith.

LOLITA

I've got a new attitude

As Lolita was driving to Greenhills, she was getting all excited because this upcoming weekend was the grand opening of her new boutique, Lolita's. She was so excited that she could hardly contain herself. "I am finally seeing my dream come true. I am going to own my own business." Her dream coming true was bitter sweet especially the way she ended up getting it.

"I had to go through a painful divorce, find out who I am in God and move on with my life at this late chapter in my life. Oh well, better late than never."

As Lolita pulled into the parking lot of her new store, she could see her name at the top and she got excited all over again. Her boutique specialized in classy dresses, suits, scarves, and handbags for corporate women. Lolita had always had impeccable taste when it came to clothing and putting pieces together. She had been to New York and Miami and even took a quick trip to Paris to pick up some of the pieces for her boutique. She had also hired an assistant and another young lady to help in the store. She wanted the ladies in Nashville to have a unique shopping experience.

So, when ladies arrived with their girlfriends, there was a quaint lounge area for guests to sit while their friends tried on their pieces of clothing. The ladies would then be offered a class of wine or champagne while they waited. There was a catwalk so that when the women came out of the dressing room, they would literally think they were modeling the pieces like they were at fashion week in New York or Paris. She wanted the ladies to have pieces that no one else in Nashville carried. She had even designed a couple of pieces herself and found a local seamstress to put them together for her. She had ordered special gift bags with her store name on the outside. Everything about her boutique screamed elegance and with the high-end clientele in Nashville, she just needed to get her name out there. She and Shelby used to shop together but since everything had happened, they no longer got together for their weekly shopping sprees and lunch. This was the part that she hated the most that she and Shelby had forgiven each other but it seemed like things would never be the same. Their relationship had been fractured severely and she really didn't know how to get it back to the way it used to be, nor did she think that she had the time or energy to try right now.

"Lord, it's going to take a miracle for Shelby and me to ever be back on the same page." Lolita had learned through her counseling that everyone has insecurities and it's up to each one of us to try to overcome those insecurities with the help of God. She was working on her insecurity issues as well as relying on God to mend and heal her one day at a time. She wasn't sure what Shelby was doing with her life right now. She ended up going by Big Mama's house every Sunday after service, but Shelby always had a reason why she couldn't come by or she would stop by after Lolita had left.

"Well, that's not my issue to try and figure out and I am going to keep moving forward with my life. I can't live my life out of my rear-view mirror anymore. I have to keep moving forward with my life. God has so much more in store for me and I can't wait until he takes me to my destiny." As Lolita walked into her boutique, it was breathtaking. The furniture, the chandelier, the catwalk, everything had been meticulously designed and no cost was spared.

"If I am going to have a boutique out here in Greenhills, I have to hang with the big dogs or stay on the porch and I have no intentions of staying on the porch another day of my life." Lolita had sent out postcards to other local merchants as well as residents in the area, advertised in the Nashville Scene and the Nashville Business Journal and one of the local magazines had done a spread on Lolita's. So now all she had to do was wait for opening day. All of her designer pieces had arrived, her wine, champagne, and even door prizes were all in place just waiting for the big day. Lolita could hardly believe her eyes, this is really happening.

"God, I am so thankful for this opportunity and I pray and ask that you also enable me to bless some women that are not so fortunate. It was as if a light had gone off in Lolita's head. That's it, Lord, I will donate a percentage of my earnings to help other women get back on their feet. I will start a non-profit once I am up and running to give back to other women. It will be called Lolita's Ladies. Thank you, Lord, for giving me the idea to own my own business and to bless others. I have so many ideas but this one will bless my soul more so than any. I don't ever want to be selfish again and only think about myself and my family. I want to show love to others like you have shown to me. This will help ladies who think that they can't make it on their own or have low self-confidence. I will even share my testimony if it will help another woman get out of a bad marriage or bad relationship. Yes, that's what I am going to do – share my blessings with others."

SHELBY

And the beat goes on

Shelby was miserable living in the house with James. "I feel like a prisoner and I can't do anything without James giving me the third degree every time I leave the house. This is getting to be ridiculous and he is working my nerves with all of this mess." Suddenly, Shelby heard her phone buzzing in her purse and picked it up and answered.

"Hello, hey baby, how are you doing?" It was Rashad.

"I'm okay. What about you?"

"I'm making it, but I would be doing much better if you were here with me Shelby. When are you going to decide? It has been over a year now and I am still waiting on you. Don't you realize how much I love you Shelby and how much you mean to me? No other man would be willing to wait on a woman the way I have waited on you."

"I know that, Rashad, and I truly appreciate you, but...."

"But what Shelby, why can't you just make a decision already? You say that you still love me and that you have never stopped loving me but we're still not together. I'm living away from you, my daughter, my family just because of you."

"Rashad, please try and understand."

"Understand what Shelby? You need to decide whether you still love me and want to be with me or if you are going to continue to be a prisoner in your house with James? I love you Shelby and I don't know what else I can do to prove that to you. I have waited all this time to be with you and marry you and now you are delaying everything. We could be a year into our marriage right now, but you are still twiddling your thumbs. I thought that after everything was out in the open, that it would make your decision easier, but I see that hasn't happened yet. I am coming to Nashville this weekend and I want to see you so that we can talk. Shelby, I really miss you, but I am not going to continue putting my life on hold because you can't make up your mind about what you want to do. I plan to see you this weekend and you can give me your answer as to whether we are going to be together or whether we will be moving on without each other. Shelby, if you tell me that you can't be with me, then that will be it. I won't see you ever again. I can't take it that you keep breaking my heart and I deserve better. I will make reservations for dinner on Friday night, so I don't know what you will tell James or tell James and he can join us but either way this weekend you are going to give me an answer and that's final." Rashad hung up the phone so abruptly and hard it scared her.

Shelby always liked it when Rashad took charge, but she didn't like the fact that he was now giving her an ultimatum. Who did he think he was giving her an ultimatum? Shelby knew what she wanted to do in her heart, but it just didn't seem to be the right time. She knew that she really did want to be with Rashad and that she still loved him. She didn't want to argue and fight with James any longer and she didn't want to remain a prisoner in her own house.

"I have a lot of thinking to do between now and Friday, so I better figure out something." Shelby had been stashing money away in her own private bank account for a rainy day over the years and she had a nice nest egg set aside that she was sure that James didn't know about. She had put the account in her name and with Big Mama's name like she was managing Big Mama's affairs. She knew that Rashad had a great income and of course she had already calculated how much alimony and child support she could get from James if she decided to leave, but he reminded her that she would leave without her children. This was the part that was not fair. She knew that she had messed up, but James had no right to tell her that she couldn't have her children and that he wanted sole custody. Just because she had an affair, it didn't make her a bad mother. She loved her children, but never thought about how any of this would affect them if she and Rashad were found out and never in a million years did she think that James would keep her children away from her. Their beautiful home was nothing more than a cold house now because there was no form of love except the love that was shown to their children. She and James rarely spoke to one another. They pretended to be the happy couple when they were at sporting events, church, or school functions with the kids, but it was all a lie. She was living a lie because she wanted to keep a certain lifestyle. She put on her "happy mask" out in public for appearance sake. It seemed that everyone else was moving on with life and she was stuck in an episode of the Twilight Zone trying to escape. The tribe meeting was tomorrow evening and she would discuss her dilemma with other members of the tribe even though she had missed the last couple of tribe meetings. She didn't feel like being preached to, stared at, or talked to anymore about the subject, but she knew that she needed some wisdom in the matter.

"Maybe, I will just call and talk to Sister Lula by myself. I truly love and respect her and I need some wise women in my life right now." She didn't want to discuss the issue anymore with Big Mama but wanted an outsider's point of view.

DEACON JONES

For Granted

As Deacon Jones was preparing to get ready for the weekend tribe meeting, he realized that he and Sister Lula hadn't prepared their lesson for the week. He always looked forward to spending some time studying the Bible with Sister Lula. She was such a joy to be around and he felt that so many of the younger women in the tribe as well as in the congregation could learn so much from her. She was the epitome of the Proverbs 31 woman and she carried herself with such grace and elegance. He didn't think that there was a mean or selfish bone in her body. She often reminded Deacon Jones that she was older than him, but, as the young people say, age was nothing, but a number and he didn't pay attention to her silliness about their age. They enjoyed each other's company and sharing with one another; sometimes about their deceased spouses.

It was nice to have Sister Lula around to chat with and to go to church functions with instead of sitting alone or feeling like a third wheel. Deacon was convinced that he could fall in love again but was hesitant because a lot of times, he would find himself comparing Lula to Mona. No one could compete with a dead spouse no matter how hard they tried. Deacon couldn't tell if he enjoyed spending time with Lula because he never spent time with Mona and this is what he could have had or the fact that this was a new relationship and it made him feel young and vibrant. He wasn't exactly sure what he was feeling and why. Lula often reminded him that they both had a call on their lives and she was in his life to let him know that you are never too old for God to use for kingdom building or sharing your testimony. She believed that once your purpose has been fulfilled then that's normally when God called you home. She often reminded him that as much as they enjoyed spending time together, their focus was to be on the Lord and Savior Jesus Christ and sharing him with the world. Lula really helped him stay on track and that was one of the things that he loved about her. He often wondered if she were not part of his life this past year would he be this far in his walk with the Lord.

He realized that his children had their own lives to live and he would see them periodically throughout the week or maybe on the weekend. He was spending more time with his children and grandchildren like never before. Mona had begged him to spend time with the family and he didn't because he was hanging out with his friends in the streets. He had brought Lula along with him to one of the grandchildren's games, but he didn't feel that his children nor the grand children were ready for him to be dating so he kept quiet and introduced Lula as one of his prayer partners. He could tell it made his children a bit uneasy, so he didn't push the issue or try and explain it to them. His children didn't realize how lonely he was at home, but he guessed that was his punishment for not being home when he had the opportunity to do so for years and took it for granted. If only he had learned these lessons years ago. He wouldn't be trying to make up for lost time. If he were only able to turn back time and start over again.

He thought about times when he had gotten drunk and done things that he shouldn't have done. He vaguely remembers one night he had too much to drink and ended up with a woman whose name he didn't even remember. He just remembered that she was being beautiful and shapely and that she had flirted with him. He had a wonderful night of lust and passion and then he never saw her again. Deacon thought it was weird that he remembered only bits and pieces of that night and found it odd that he never saw her again. Maybe she was out for the night trying to forget her home life like he was doing. He knew that his home life wasn't bad, he was just bored with it. That was just a different time in his life and he was glad that he had moved past all his foolishness.

SANIYA

Living life

As Saniya was piddling around upstairs in her room, she heard the home phone ring and her mother answer.

"Saniya, telephone."

"Who is it?"

"May I ask who is calling?"

"It's Micah."

"Okay ask him to hold on for a moment, I will be right down." Saniya ran down the stairs but tried to keep her composure as she answered the phone.

"Hello, hey Saniya, how are you?"

"I'm good and you?"

"I can't complain. I was just wondering whether or not you were going to give me your address so that I could come by and pick you up?"

"Oh, my God, I am sorry, I forgot to give you the most important piece of information." It must be those gray eyes Saniya was thinking to herself. She had tried to keep cool whenever she talked to Micah or saw him at work, but she did realize that he was FINE with capital letters. She was trying not to get too excited, but it was hard to do whenever she saw him. She gave Micah her address and he told her what time he was picking her up for the movies. She was getting excited and trying to decide what to wear.

"Micah, huh?" Her mother said smiling at her in the midst of her excitement.

"Well, Mama, you told me to find some balance and get out of the house some, so I am taking your advice."

"Lord, let me write this down if you are listening to me." They both laughed at her mother's comment. Suddenly, the phone rang again, and Saniya grabbed it thinking that Micah had forgot to tell her something. But when she answered, it was Xavier.

"Hey Saniya, what are you up to?"

"Xavier!" Saniya said sharply.

"Please don't hang up."

"What do you want, Xavier? I'm about to get ready to go out with some friends from work."

"That's nice. I was just sitting here thinking about you and wanted to call and check on you." Saniya could feel her heart softening, so she said, "I have just been studying, working, and trying to spend some time with my family and friends – You?"

"Not much. I am playing at a new church so when I'm not working, I'm either at choir practice, skating or shooting hoops with the boys. Saniya, I really miss you and would hope that one day, we can be friends again and maybe even get back together." There was a long moment of silence. Saniya didn't know what to say.

"Well maybe one day but I don't know when that will be

Xavier." She could feel her eyes start to water so she said, "Well, I have to go get ready so I can head out. Thanks for calling to check on me." She hung up quickly.

Her mother was watching and asked sweetly, "Are you okay baby?"

"Yes Mama, I'm okay."

Her mama grabbed her and said, "You don't miss your good thing until it's gone. Even though Xavier was not my favorite person or the guy that I would have chosen for you, I believe that he did love you and care about you and I believe you had the same feelings and possibly still do. But you need to let this play out and you need to go out and enjoy yourself. After all, if he truly loves you, then he will come back to you and you will know it and if God means for you to be together, then you will be together. Now, get your face all dolled up and get ready. I can't wait to meet this new guy." Saniya blushed and kissed her Mama.

Saniya went upstairs and started getting ready and when she was finishing her makeup and hair, she heard the doorbell ring.

"Hello Micah, please come in, nice to meet you. Saniya, Micah is here. Have a seat Micah, I'm Saniya's Mother, Samantha."

"Nice to meet you ma'am."

"Nice to meet you as well. Let me go upstairs and let Saniya know you are here. Would you like something to drink?"

"No ma'am, I'm fine." Saniya's Mother made her way up

the stairs and knocked on her door and barged into the room.

"Saniya are you ready?"

"Yes ma'am. I'm just touching up my lipstick."

"Chile, why didn't you tell me that boy was that fine?"

"Mama!" Saniya exclaimed.

"Mama nothing, hell I would go out with him if I wasn't old enough to be his mother. You should be saying Xavier who?"

"Mama stop it!" Saniya said blushing.

"Whatever Saniya, that boy is FINE with capital letters and has good manners."

"Of course, he does Mama, this is his first time meeting you."

They looked at each other and they both laughed. Her mother walked back downstairs with her leading the way like she was leading her daughter down the aisle for marriage. Saniya could see her Mama's mind spinning while she was looking at Micah and at her.

"Well Mama, we are headed out, so we will see you later."

"Okay, Micah it was nice meeting you.

"Likewise, Mrs. Samantha."

Her mother smiled at her and mouthed, "Don't do anything that I wouldn't do." Saniya had never seen her mother act like that before. You would have thought that Micah was taking her out on the date. Saniya laughed to herself thinking, "Well you got my Mama's attention then you must be fine." She knew her Mother was acting silly and she had fun with it. Maybe I will sit back and enjoy this night after all."

"Saniya, do you like Eddie Murphy? He is starring in a new movie called Coming to America."

"Yes, I would love to see it."

"I was hoping you would say that. He is one of the funniest comedians out right now. I can always use some laughs and with school and work, I'm sure you could also."

"Yes, I agree with you on that one Micah. Let's take a break from reality." As Micah got out of the car, he came around and opened her door and as they began to walk toward the theater, he grabbed her hand and looked at her and smiled. Saniya could feel her face getting hot.

"I hope you don't mind, do you?"

"No, not at all," Saniya said blushing, "Not at all." Even though she was here with this fine brotha and planned on having an enjoyable night, Xavier had invaded her thoughts and her heart with his phone call saying that he missed her.

ISLAND

Miami Bound

As Island checked out his beachfront condo, he decided that life was good. One thing about working for a large corporation, they didn't cut corners on taking good care of their employees when they had to travel or be displaced.

"I believe I could start enjoying this Miami beach life." Of course, he knew it was just the newness of everything and being in a new city; a change of atmosphere. He had learned over the last couple of years to be content with what he already had in life and to stop looking for adventure in the streets and in the bedroom. He had come to realize that he had a void in his life that only God could fill, and he was filling himself up with a lot of God lately. Before leaving to come to Miami, Pastor Harris had given him the names of a couple of churches in the area along with a friend of his that he could call in the event he needed someone locally to talk to while in Miami. Island appreciated Pastor Harris, Deacon Jones and his counselor and all that they had done to help him. They were being father figures to him and he had much love and respect for them. It was so much easier when they were around and now here he was alone without them nearby to help him. He hoped that he could remain strong in their absence. He had learned that not every man in a position of authority was bad or out to harm him. He was learning to trust again – which had been an issue for him all these years – so he was making progress.

Island decided to get comfortable and take a stroll on the beach. As the sun was about to set, he saw couple after couple holding hands and laughing as they strolled along the beach in the warm white sand. As the beautiful turquoise water and the blue sky seemed to touch one another and with the warm colors of the sun setting over the clear water, Island was in awe of what God was doing right in front of his eyes to close out the day. The colors of the sun setting over the ocean were amazing, and Island thought about how he wished he had someone to spend evenings like this with instead of being alone. He had learned to enjoy being alone and spending time with God recently and just looked at this as another opportunity to strengthen his relationship with God and dive deeper into His word. After watching the beautiful rays of red, orange, and yellow disappear over the horizon Island decided to continue his stroll to his condominium and get ready for dinner.

"I am going to get out my linen for tonight and kill em with my Miami Vice look," he thought as he laughed aloud at himself. Island knew he looked good in linen and had turned several heads anytime he wore his linen suit.

"If a handsome brotha like myself can't pull off wearing linen and looking good; there's something wrong." The last time Island wore his linen suit, he got so many numbers he didn't know where to start. He had decided to get rid of all of them so that he could stay out of trouble. Suddenly Island heard his cell phone ringing and answered. It was his partner Reggie on the other end of the line asking him the name of the restaurant where they were meeting for dinner.

"Man don't worry about it; the company is having a car pick us up and drive us to dinner. I just know that I want me some good Cuban food while I'm here but of course I will be able to try a variety of foods since we will be here for a few months."

"Man, I can't wait to see some of these honeys here in Miami," Reggie said enthusiastically.

"Oh boy, here you go. The first night out and you already on patrol." They both laughed.

"Hey, I don't want to deprive the Miami ladies of all of this chocolate goodness man. So, you feel like hitting one of the hot spots with me tonight after dinner?"

"Man, I don't know, I will probably come back to the condo and chill since we have to hit the ground running on Monday morning."

"That's why they are splurging on us this weekend, man, because they know once we start on Monday, we will have our noses to the grindstone for months trying to get this office up and running in such a short amount of time. You know that there are haters in the office that want us to fail, so we have got to succeed so that we can prove them wrong."

"I know what you mean Reggie. It seems like there's always somebody out to get you or haters wanting to see you fail and it is normally the people that you wouldn't suspect.

Sometimes it's our own folks that do us in and I'm not just talking about Black folks, I'm also talking about "Christian" folks. Maybe one of these days, we as a race will get rid of that crab mentality and be able to uplift one another and work together and stop being so fearful that somebody else is going to have more than you do. It is so sad, and you get sick of it — the envy, jealousy, and hatred. It's hard for a brotha out here in corporate America trying to make a living. At the end of the day some of these people in our office don't want a brotha telling them what to do. I can have degrees from the most prestigious university in the United States and they still want to question a brotha about the decisions that you make. Man, the struggle is real but at the end of the day, we have to remember that God has our back."

"Oh, there you go throwing God in the midst of our conversation."

"Reggie, you need some God in your conversations the way you are living foul," Island said laughing.

"Okay, Mr. Music Director/future Vice President, why you got to talk trash to a brotha?"

"I'm just saying Reggie, I want you to have a serious relationship with God like I have been encountering with Him over the last couple of years."

"Man, I'm only 30 years old, I have plenty of time to get it right with God so until then, I am going to party and have myself a good time. I will see you downstairs at 8:00 – Later."

As they arrived at the Cuban restaurant that Island's boss had told them about, the wonderful aromas of ethnic food made Island's mouth water. "I can't wait to throw down up in here; it smells divine up in this place. I want a little bit of everything. I want some Ropa Viejo, some rice and black beans and a nice Mojito to complete an amazing meal."

"Hold up church boy, are you supposed to have alcohol?"

"Where in the Bible do you see that having a drink will send you to hell? It's all good Reggie, alcohol is not my stumbling block. I can have a drink or two and it's okay to do things in moderation, not excessively."

"Worldly folks always want to cast a stone at a Christian if they "think" they are doing something wrong. The word said in Ephesians 5:18 and Galatians 5:32 not to get in a drunken state, that's when you get into trouble." Island often used opportunities like these to teach Reggie the word.

Island knew this place was going to be good because it was packed full of people and people only come to a good restaurant if the food is good and worth the wait. As the group laughed and talked about the upcoming week and all the work that they had to do, Island thought he heard a familiar voice but dismissed it. As he excused himself from the table and walked toward the men's room, he heard his name.

"Island, Island, hey Island." When he turned around, he couldn't believe his eyes. "Taylor, "what are you doing here?"

"Nice to see you too, Island," she said. All in a moment, Island's mind was flooded with thoughts that took him to places he didn't want to go to.

"Wow imagine running into you here in Miami." Island said.

"How have you been?" Taylor asked.

"Uhhh, I'm good, no complaints. I am here for the next few months working and setting up a satellite office for the company."

"And you?"

"I'm good, staying busy with work. I will be doing some interior decorating for a new office building that is opening in the next few months." Taylor responded.

"That wouldn't happen to be the office building called the Hightower Building, would it?"

"Yes, it is," she responded.

"Wow, I can't believe this, that is where our new office will be located." There was an awkward moment of silence as Island looked at Taylor. She was still one of the most beautiful women that he had ever known. Taylor was a mocha color girl with jet black hair which she always wore in a sassy, short style and she had the body of a sistah to die for. She had curves in all the right places with the most beautiful dark eyes and luscious lips that he had ever kissed. She was looking at him as well, but he couldn't tell what she was thinking.

"Well, maybe we can get together for lunch or dinner while we are both down here working. I won't mind being here instead of New York now that winter is fast approaching."

"Me either, although in Tennessee we do have a beautiful fall of the year, but I will take the ocean any day."

"It was really good seeing you, Island. You look great."
Taylor reached over and gave him a hug, handed him her
business card and walked away.

"Taylor."

She turned around.

"Yes, Island."

"I just want to say that it was good seeing you and...." She
cut him off and shook her head and said, "We are not going
back down that road, not tonight," and she walked away.
Island stood there for a moment until he realized that this
was the woman that he had loved and wanted to marry and
ruined the relationship with his issues. He wasn't sure how
he felt now. Part of him was happy that he had seen her and
part of him was sad for the pain and hurt he had caused her
and himself. He went on to the bathroom and then headed
back to the table to finish the night off.

"Island are you okay?" Reggie asked.

"Yeah, yeah, I'm good."

"Who was that fine sistah that I saw you talking to?"

"That was my former girlfriend, Taylor."

"What? Man, you let that go? You must be out your mind.
Do you want anything to drink Island other than water?"

"Yeah, I will have another mojito". He tried to pay
attention to the conversation, but his focus was on seeing
Taylor and wondering why or how he could have run into
her in Miami. Seeing her flooded him with all kinds of
emotions. He wasn't sure how to handle them, so he
ordered another Mojito. And then another.

LOLITA

Grand Opening

Lolita's grand opening had been a huge success and her weekend was unbelievable. She had a lot of traffic in her boutique for the weekend – the elegant ladies of Nashville really showed up and showed out. She had sold several of her designer pieces and heard all kinds of nice comments from the ladies who came into the boutique. Shelby had even come in for the grand opening, although Lolita didn't really get to chat with her because the store was so busy. The Tennessean and the Nashville Scene had been there with their photographers, so Lolita was over the moon. Shelby mingled in with the crowd and smiled at Lolita a couple of times, but Lolita could tell that Shelby was not happy. There was something missing from her eyes. She just looked empty.

"I don't know why I am trying to feel sorry for my sister, but I am. Even after all the dirt she has done and all the wrong she has done to me, I do feel bad for her." Lolita's assistant called to her and told her that she had a delivery. When she came out to the front of the store, there was a beautiful bouquet of flowers waiting for her.

"Oh, my goodness, where did these come from?"

"Well, there's a card. Do you want me to open it or do you want to open it?"

"No, you open it," Lolita told her assistant. She pulled the card from the flowers and read it aloud. "Congratulations on your grand opening. I just wanted to let you know how proud I am of you and what you have accomplished – Rashad."

"Rashad?"

"Yes, that's what the card says."

"Wow, that was awful sweet of him. In the back of her mind, Lolita was wondering what Rashad was up to, but then again, she really didn't care anymore about what he was doing. Whatever he was doing was his business. Lolita had learned to mind her own business and stay in her lane and only be concerned about her life and her family.

"Leave those out on the counter so that we can enjoy them this week. I'm headed back to my office to do the books before we close today." As Lolita arrived back at her office, she heard the bell in the front of the store ring and heard her assistant tell the customer that they were still open and would be closing within the hour.

"Please feel free to browse around."

Lolita heard a man's voice and a woman's voice and heard the man say, "This hat looks just like something that Mama would love to have." The female laughed and agreed with him.

"Of course, she would because she has impeccable tastes and so does whoever owns this boutique. They have some fabulous pieces and I see several that I would like to have. Too bad they don't have men's clothing brother but please feel free to come in and shop for me and Mama anytime. I love stores like this where you can find unusual pieces that you won't find anywhere else. There's nothing worse than going somewhere and seeing someone in the same outfit that you have on – uuuuggghhh. If the owner continues to carry pieces like this, I won't have to fly to New York or Chicago for the day and do shopping, I can just come in here. That would save the hubby some money," she laughed. About that time Lolita came out of the back of the store to speak to her customers and when the man turned around, she realized it was the guy from church that spoke to her last Sunday.

"Well hello there, imagine seeing you here?" he said in his Dennis Haysbert voice.

"Well, you should since this is my store. Hi, my name is Lolita Jones."

"Nice to meet you Lolita, I'm Aiden Harper and I saw you last Sunday at service. This is my sister Alicia."

"Nice to meet you Alicia."

"Lolita, you have some exquisite pieces here in your boutique. I love the styles you have here."

"Thanks, I picked up some pieces in New York and in Paris and I have designed a few of the pieces myself."

"Well, I was just telling Aiden that our Mother would love your store." Lolita was checking out Aiden along with Alicia. Both were dressed to the nines and Aiden reminded her of Denzel Washington. He was about 6'3" with curly black hair and a smile to die for. He was built nicely and appeared to be an avid runner and probably daily workout guy and the cologne he was wearing was surfacing in Lolita's nostrils and making her lose focus.

"Well, Lolita, we are going to get these two pieces and get out of here, so you ladies can close down for the night."

"I really appreciate you stopping in. Let us gift wrap your items for you, Lolita's assistant, Monique said. "I will be back in a few minutes."

"Lolita, can I browse around a few more minutes while we are waiting for Monique?"

"Of course, you can, let me show you around."

"No, you go ahead and do whatever you need to do. I can come back another day when you're not about to close." About that time Monique resurfaced and called Alicia to hand her the items she had wrapped.

"Aiden, it was nice putting a name with a face. How long have you been coming to New Divine Fellowship?"

"I've only been there about a month. I have to travel sometimes for work, so I may miss service but trust me when I'm in town, I do make it to get a word. Pastor Harris brings the word and makes it understandable." "You?"

"Oh, I have been there for a few years now. I did miss some this past year due to some personal issues, but I'm back in the groove of things."

"Glad to hear it. So, let me grab my sister so we can get out of here. I look forward to seeing you at service on Sunday or around town" he said smiling at her.

"Likewise," Lolita said blushing.

"I hope so." Lolita hadn't blushed over a man in some time. She wasn't sure how to handle these warm and fuzzy feelings that were rising within her body. Of course, she knew what she was feeling was hormonal and the word began with lust and not love. She hadn't had another man's attention in years and if she wasn't mistaken, Mr. Aiden was kinda flirting with her.

"Oh, stop it," she said to herself. "There I go fantasizing about a man that I just met, and he could just be being nice." I am probably reading way too much into his kindness." One of the things that Lolita had learned in her therapy sessions was how young girls watch the movies where a man comes in and saves them from everything. You have to realize that you may have an episode of nightmare on Elm Street or One Flew Over the Cuckoo's Nest. People tell you that marriage is not easy, but you never think the bad stuff will happen to you. It's hard handling the stuff in between. All you read in books and see in the movies is the damsel in distress, the prince charming guy coming in to save her and then they get married and live happily ever after.

"Somebody better teach these girls that there is a lot of stuff in between until you get to the happily ever after." Lolita was going to be sure and teach her daughter that marriage is not a bed of roses or a happily ever after. She wanted her to have a reality of what marriage is all about as well as the flip side of divorce and the pain it causes. Sometimes in life bad stuff happens to good people. As Lolita was finishing after Aiden and Alicia left the store, she heard her cell phone ringing.

"Hello"

Yes, this is she. What? When? What hospital? Okay, I'm on my way." "Monique," Lolita yelled, "I have a family emergency, I have to go! Can you close up?"

Monique came in running and said, "Do you need for me to drive you?"

"No, I will be okay" as Lolita darted out the door.

"Call my sister and tell her to meet me at the emergency room at Centennial Medical Center and hurry."

SHELBY

Who will I run to?

"Thanks for meeting with me, Sister Lula. I needed a wise female to talk to me about this whole mess that I have created for myself and my family. I also want to thank you so much for all the love that you have shown me and my sister over the last year or so. You have been so kind to both of us and I'm sure that there have been times that you all wanted to throw us over your knees and beat some sense into us both." Sister Lula chuckled.

"I didn't say that, you did. Yes Shelby, it has been an interesting year with you and Lolita. I have done a great deal of praying for both of you and I have been praying that your relationship as sisters will be restored. That you both will find forgiveness in your hearts for one another and what you have done to each other. You know that there is responsibility to be had by both of you and let's not leave out Rashad. The sad thing is that both of you have children that have been involved in all this mess. They had no part in any of this, but they are the ones that suffer."

"I suffer as well, Sister Lula."

"Shelby, this is not about you. It's about how your actions

have affected the people in your life that love you and care about you. It's about James and your children. The whole situation is messy, and it probably wouldn't be as bad if your children were adults, but you have young, impressionable children. You all will have to be careful how you handle this situation going forward because they are watching your every move."

"Sister Lula, I still love Rashad and I can't imagine my life without him. We have been a part of each other's lives for so long that I don't know how I would breathe without him and I have been miserable since he left town. I feel like a prisoner in my own house and I say house because it is no longer a home. It's cold and dreary like someone has sucked all the love and the air out of the place. James questions me like he's the FBI on whatever I am doing, and we sleep in separate bedrooms. We live in the same house, but it just seems like we are roommates at this point and time."

"Shelby, I'm not sure what you were expecting to happen after all of this blew up, but you should be thankful that you are still in your marriage, have your children and a place to stay."

"I am thankful, but I don't feel like I should be punished for the rest of my life either."

"Have you sat down with James and talked to him?"

"I have tried, and he pretty much doesn't want to hear anything that I have to say. Rashad called me earlier this week and he will be in town tonight and wants an answer from me as to whether I am going to be with him and marry him or stay with James. I don't know what to do Sister Lula.

I'm torn between the man I love and staying in a miserable marriage for the sake of my children."

"Have you sat down and talked with the children about any of this? I believe that you will be able to get some insight on how they feel about you and James and they are old enough to make a decision as to who they would want to live with."

"That's what I'm afraid of. What if they want to stay with James? I'm a good mother if nothing else Sister Lula and I love my children."

"Well, then you need to fight for your children, Shelby, and don't just give up. It sounds like you truly love Rashad, and nobody can tell your heart any different. I truly believe that James is hurt and taking all his anger and frustration out on you by threatening you with your children but one day, he will move past his pain and continue living life again. I'm not saying that I agree with anything that has transpired between you and Rashad, but I do know that you are human and Christian or not, we all make mistakes. We're not perfect but we're forgiven. I don't agree with how you all handled things, but since you asked me I am telling you. The situation should have been handled years ago if all of you had been honest with one another but don't miss the opportunity to make things right with those you love. Apologize and ask for forgiveness. Make sure you read 1 Corinthians 13 about what love is Shelby, and make sure that it is really love that you are feeling toward Rashad. God is love and we have to look at Him and His word to truly see what love is. Sometimes, we as women look for what we think love should be, not what love really is. We also fall in love with men that we think can make us whole or fill in the gap that was left by an absent father. We have to realize that the first man that we as women look up to is our father and if you don't have a father in the house with you affirming who you are as a young lady and showing you how men are supposed to treat women then you have a problem. If you and Rashad are meant to be together, it will all work out and come together. A lot of times, the Lord has outlined our paths, but we drift away from the path that He has chosen for us and then He redirects our path and gets us back on track. Just make sure that you are hearing God speak to you, Shelby, before you change tracks."

"Yes ma'am. Thanks so much for chatting with me Sister Lula. I truly appreciate you," Shelby said goodbye and kissed Sister Lula on the cheek. Shelby was about to go out the door when her phone rang but she let it go to voicemail. She had a lot to think about before meeting Rashad.

Later that night, as Shelby arrived at the restaurant, she saw Rashad sitting in a booth in the back. She was nervous about meeting him after their earlier conversation. She could tell that he was not completely at ease because she could see the vein popping out on the side of his forehead which always meant he was stressing about something.

"Shelby, thanks for meeting me for dinner," he said abruptly. She knew from his tone that he was still caught up in his feelings, so she was going to tread lightly.

"Shelby, I have been dying to see you and I'm not going to continue playing this waiting game another day with you.

You need to make a decision!" Shelby could feel her heart beating. Deep down she loved Rashad and he was the only man that she had ever truly loved deeply and been totally honest and transparent with in her life.

"Rashad," but before she could finish her sentence and sit down, he grabbed her and kissed her passionately. When Shelby opened her eyes, he pulled out her chair for her to sit down as well.

"Tell me that you don't feel the same way about me Shelby and I will walk out of this restaurant right now!"

"I do love you."

"Well, that settles it then Shelby we need to move forward with our lives and stop wasting time. I love you and there's nothing you can say or do that will change that, but I don't want to keep putting my life on hold any longer without you. If I need to help you with your divorce, then I will do it. If I need to help you with talking to James, then I will do it. Whatever you need for me to do, I'm here for you Shelby. Everything is out in the open and there are no more secrets to keep from James or your family and hopefully, we all will be able to move forward with our lives and stop making each other miserable."

"I have made up my mind, Rashad, and I must tell you that I am terrified at the decision that I am about to make." About that time Shelby's phone rang. She hit the button for it to go to voicemail, but it immediately rang again.

"Rashad, I better take this since they called right back. Hold on one second." Rashad looked agitated but didn't say anything.

"Hello, yes this is she. Who is this? Why are you calling me?" Rashad could tell by Shelby's tone of voice that something was wrong.

"Oh my God, I'm on the way. Rashad, I have to go, I have a family emergency and I have to get to Centennial Medical Center. It's Big Mama."

"Come on, I will drive you I don't want you driving upset like this" and they both ran out of the restaurant.

DEACON JONES

Trials and Tribulations

Deacon Jones had been calling Sister Lula all morning but hadn't been able to reach her. "Well, she may be out and about with her sisters hanging out. I am going to go and see my children and grand babies and spend some time with them today and I will buzz Lula later."

He and Sister Lula had talked on the phone last night on over into the night about the Bible, how God had kept them all these years and through difficult times, and how they needed to continue to share with the young people like they had been commissioned. Without sharing details, Sister Lula shared that she had a conversation with Shelby and that she hoped that Shelby understood what she was saying to her. Deacon Jones also shared with Sister Lula how important it was for men to be the fathers that God had called them to be and that some of the decisions that women made were possibly the reflection of some of the things that the fathers did or didn't do in the young lady's lives.

"Lula, we have to understand how important our role is in our daughter's lives. Even though I wasn't the best husband, I always tried to be available to my children and let them know that I loved them. I may not have been there for all the practices, but I made it a point to show up for their games and what was important to them. I know that there is more that I could have done. I am now trying to make up for some of the things now. I can also make a difference in the lives of my grandchildren."

They talked about forgiveness and the importance of forgiveness in our lives. "It's not for the other person but for us and the Lord tells us that if we don't forgive, then He can't forgive us." *Matthew 6:15.* Sister Lula and Deacon Jones were able to talk for hours and then they also talked about how their latter days were supposed to be better than their former days like the Lord promised. *Job 8:7* Sister Lula said that her latter days had been filled with joy and happiness, even though she had been widowed for some time. She spent so much time in the presence of the Lord that she knew that He was always with her and that He had taken care of her over the years. She had relayed this information to her family whenever they worried about her – – that God had kept her through good times and bad times and that she had learned to totally depend and trust Him for everything. She thanked Deacon Jones for his company and their walks and talks together, sharing with one another.

"I have really enjoyed our time together and look forward to us continuing to share with these young folks. They need us for such a time as this. This world has gone crazy and there are times that you are just ready for the Lord to come on back because there is so much evil in this world."

"I appreciate you too, Deacon, and the time we have been

spending together talking and reminiscing about old times and also cutting up with these young folks."

"What a glorious day it will be when we get to see the Lord face to face," Sister Lula told Deacon, "What a day it will be. We must always be ready. Make sure that you thank the Lord every day that you open your eyes and that you don't take anything or anyone for granted."

"Well then Lula, I need to let you know how much I truly appreciate you and your friendship over the last year or so. I never knew that I could have such a great friend of the opposite sex and not have a woman after me for my money or material things. When you're in the streets doing all manner of things, the women are looking at what you have and what you can do for them.

Deacon Jones told her he now understood how precious life really is, but he still had a hard time saying goodbye.

"It's never easy Deacon but it's not goodbye, it's until I see you again because we will all be together again." They had laughed and joked some more and then finally hung up the phone. They were like two teenagers talking on the phone and could go on and on with one another, but both knew it was past their bedtime and they laughed even more before finally hanging up.

As Deacon Jones returned home that night from spending time with his children and grandchildren he was getting sleepy. "Oh, let me call Lula before I turn in for the night since I haven't talked to her today." Deacon Jones called, and the phone just rang and rang.

"That's odd, he thought, I know that Lula is not out this

late but maybe she has already turned in for the night. I guess I will just have to check in with her on tomorrow."

No sooner than Deacon turned off his light and dozed off, his phone rang.

"Hello?"

"Hello, Deacon."

"Pastor Harris, what are you doing up so late?" Deacon Jones could hear Rev. Harris speaking but it was like he couldn't grasp what he was saying. He thought that Pastor Harris said something about Sister Lula, but it couldn't be what he thought he said.

"Oh my God! Are you serious? Oh Lord, I can't take this right now!" Deacon Jones could hear Pastor Harris calling his name, but he was unable to respond. All he could do was start crying uncontrollably. He felt himself sliding down onto the floor. He couldn't believe the words that he had just heard. About that time there was a knock at his door.

"Deacon Jones, it's Pastor Harris." Deacon was able to bring himself to get up and answer the door and when he did Pastor Harris could tell that the news that he had just relayed to him had been devastating. He was glad that he decided to head to Deacon Jones' house while he had him on the phone.

"Deacon, I was trying to get to you without telling you on the phone, but you answered so suddenly. I know that you are startled over the news like all of us and it has been a shock to you, but I want you to know that it was very peaceful."

"Pastor I don't know if I can take this, this is too much.

I can't believe that Lula has went on to be with the Lord. We were just talking last night. We were reminiscing and sharing about the goodness of the Lord, forgiveness our purpose in life and so forth. This is too much and not to mention, I was really starting to have feelings for her. She's such a jewel. I mean, she was such a jewel. Lord, why her?" Deacon Jones felt as if his heart would crack into a million pieces again just like a couple of years ago. Pastor Harris' phone rang, and he answered it.

"Oh, my Lord! I'm on the way. Deacon, I need for you to come with me. There's an emergency and we are needed at Centennial Medical Center." Deacon was still in shock, but he managed to shake his head, throw his clothes back on and follow Pastor Harris. He was still trying to digest the news he just received about Sister Lula.

SANIYA

Date Night

"Saniya I'm glad that you decided to go out with me to the movies. I had a really great time and I hope you enjoyed yourself as well."

"I did, you are an interesting guy, Mr. Micah, but I like it. Your friends were pretty cool as well."

"I'm glad that you feel that way. I was such a geek in high school and in my neighborhood, but I had to learn to be comfortable in my own skin. I used to get teased because I wore glasses and had braces and I stayed in the library all the time. I have always loved reading and I have always been fascinated by what I could learn next. I was bullied by other kids in the neighborhood by being called light bright almost white, white boy, et cetera just because of my looks. Once I got contact lenses and got the braces removed, it seemed like things changed. I started having girls flirt with me and then the bullying from the guys got worse because then all the girls were paying attention to me and not them. I turned it around and said hey, if you hang with me then you may be able to get some of the girls as well. I started using my looks to get my way and help other brothas out but then my Mom taught me that beauty is only skin deep. What's in your heart matters most."

She said, "Now that you have all of these girls' attention don't let that change you. Why couldn't they be interested in you when you had the glasses and the braces? You want people to love you for who you are on the inside not what you look like on the outside. Choose wisely. She then went on to explain the same lesson about women. A woman can be beautiful on the inside and be ugly in her heart."

"I tend to watch and listen and, just like Jesus told us to watch and pray, I do the same thing about dating. Sure, there were a lot of girls at the job smiling and flirting with me, but they were superficial and not real. When I spoke to you, you let me know real quick that you were about business and then I overheard you talking to one of the girls in the break room saying that you didn't have time for drama and foolishness and that spoke volumes to me. We both have bright futures ahead of us, Saniya, so I appreciate the fact that you are keeping your head straight and staying focused. I understand that we both have crazy schedules, but I hope that we will get to hang out together more."

"I totally get what you are saying, Micah. I was always self-conscious about my skin color as well. I am the total opposite of you and I didn't think of myself as beautiful because I was a dark chocolate girl and I had to learn the same lesson that it's all about the heart and what's on the inside. I also realized that there were guys that loved mocha looking girls like me as well. It's sad in our community how we hurt one another by saying ignorant things that we have had put in our heads during slavery that still exist today and keep us divided; especially our skin tones. Even the hair issue, saying she has 'good hair or that light-skinned people are better looking than dark-skinned people. This all stems from slavery times and what was taught to our race/people.' The foolishness is unbelievable, but we as a people must learn to love ourselves and stop letting others dictate what is or isn't beautiful. All that matters is what God says about us. Whenever I get married and have children, I want to enforce how important it is to love the skin you're in and that your skin color doesn't define you as a person. For far too long, our race has let other folks tell us what is beautiful. How did we ever allow another culture to define beauty for us?"

"Well you can be my coffee and I will be your cream," Micah said and they both laughed.

"We live and learn, don't we? Micah said. As they pulled up at Saniya's house, they were still laughing and talking.

"Wow, I hate to leave good company, but I know we both have service in the morning. Can I call you after I get out of service tomorrow or after I finish running errands?"

"Sure, I would love that Micah." As Saniya reached in her purse to pull out her keys, she noticed that she had a message on her phone and must not have heard the phone ringing.

"Oh boy, I missed a few calls and there is a message on my phone. Let me check right quick before I go inside if that's okay with you?"

"Sure," Micah said.

"Oh my God!" Saniya exclaimed. Micah could tell

something was wrong and he noticed Saniya's eyes watering up as she was listening to her message.

"Micah, I'm sorry but I need to go to Centennial Medical Center. My Mom is there with some of our church members and our prayer group."

"Okay, no problem, I will drive you."

As Pastor Harris and Deacon Jones arrived at the hospital, Pastor Harris saw Shelby, Lolita and then Saniya and another young man that he didn't recognize.

"Lolita, Shelby, what's going on?"

"It's Big Mama Pastor. They think that she has had a major stroke and it's not good," Lolita said beginning to cry. James had called Pastor Harris and some of the prayer warriors had started calling one another to pray and several of the members had showed up at the hospital to support Shelby and Lolita. Pastor Harris had also spotted Rashad talking with another member and he was praying that there wouldn't be any drama at the hospital, especially with Shelby and Lolita together and with Rashad and James both being there. The doctor came out of the room and told Shelby and Lolita that he needed to speak with them. He took them into a conference room and told them that Big Mama was in and out of consciousness and that she had suffered some major damage to her heart, brain and motor functions. He told them that her prognosis wasn't good and right now that they all needed to pray. He agreed to let them have some time alone with her but to make it brief. Shelby and Lolita walked into Big Mama's room together. She was hooked up to all kinds of machines. She looked so peaceful and helpless lying there and both began crying. James and Rashad both stayed in the waiting room and waited for Pastor Harris to motion for them to come into the room. James eyed Rashad as if he wanted to kill him but Rashad ignored him.

"Big Mama, you have to wake up, we need you. You are all we have left so please wake up, please don't leave us!" Lolita echoed what Shelby was saying from the other side of the bed.

"This can't be happening we just saw her a couple of days ago and she was fine." The doctor said it was sudden but that she could have been having a series of mini strokes and we didn't know it.

"Big Mama, we love you and we need you, so please hang in there."

About that time, they noticed Big Mama blinking her eyes.

"Hey there, thank God you can hear us," Lolita said. Big Mama managed a little smile and blinked twice.

"I love you too" she managed to whisper. Her speech was choppy, but they could manage to make out some of what she was saying. Big Mama managed to say, "Promise me – forgive – love." She took another breath and said "love." Each time she spoke her breathing quickened.

"Big Mama, we promise to forgive and love one another." Big Mama blinked twice again as a tear rolled down her cheeks.

"Love you both" as Shelby bent down to kiss Big Mama, she noticed that Big Mama closed her eyes and then the heart monitor went off because she had flat lined. Lolita began screaming as nurses and the doctor rushed into the room and moved her back. Lolita felt as if she was having an out of body experience and she could feel herself screaming but everything was in slow motion as she collapsed. Someone grabbed her before she hit the floor. Shelby was screaming as well. "No Big Mama, no, please stay with us!!!" Shelby felt someone grab her and hold her tight as her body went limp. The prayer warriors outside the room were praying but could hear the blood wrenching screams from Shelby and Lolita and they knew what had just happened. As the doctor came out he went to Pastor Harris and told him that Big Mama had just died. Pastor Harris grabbed Deacon Jones and they went into the room to pray with Shelby and Lolita. Everyone in the lobby was crying as well, because their hearts were broken, their congregation had received a double whammy today. Sister Lula and now Big Mama both within 24 hours.

The nurses had to administer smelling salt to Lolita because she had passed out and when she came to. Aiden next to her, holding her hand.

"Lolita, Lolita, it's going to be okay, just breathe." She felt like she was in the twilight zone and then remembered what had just happened and began sobbing again. Aiden lifter her up and sat her in the chair in the room. Lolita looked and saw Pastor Harris, Deacon Jones and then Big Mama lying in the bed looking so peaceful. She then spotted Shelby with Rashad holding her up as she was crying and

James standing in the background. Shelby had apparently collapsed as well.

"Lolita, I'm here for you if you need anything."

Aiden helped Lolita up and she walked across the room to Shelby. As Rashad noticed Lolita coming towards he and Shelby, you could tell he wasn't sure what to expect as his eyes widened. Lolita moved past him and went and grabbed Shelby and they held on to each other and sobbed uncontrollably together. Pastor Harris motioned for everyone to leave the room so that they could grieve with one another. They all made their way back into the conference room where Shelby and Lolita had met with the doctor. Pastor Harris was even choked up, but cleared his throat and said, "the last 24 hours have been a very challenging day for our congregation. In less than 24 hours, the Lord has called Sister Lula home and now Sister Imogene." Saniya and others gasped because they didn't know about Sister Lula and then there were more tears that came about from the group. Saniya looked up and thought that she even saw Xavier, but she couldn't tell through her tears. Micah was holding her tight and she welcomed the comfort of his arms. Several of the members were comforting one another. Pastor Harris asked everyone to grab hands. He started praying for the families and their church family because their hearts were broken. He reminded everyone that at some point and time in our lives, that we will have to deal with death and even though we are Christians, it is still painful because we will miss our loved ones. But as Sister Lula said, it's not goodbye but until we meet again. When Pastor Harris finished praying, they all dispersed and went their separate ways still in shock and disbelief. Saniya pulled away from Micah to go get some water and as she was walking down the hallway she thought she heard her name.

"Saniya, Saniya." Saniya turned around and saw that it was Xavier calling her name. "Hey, are you okay?" as he grabbed her and hugged her.

"No, I'm not but I will be. What are you doing here?"

"You know I loved me some Sister Lula and Sister Imogene. They were always feeding me and telling me that I better get myself together. They were some exceptional seasoned ladies and one of the members from the prayer group called me and told me what had happened, so I came right over. Do you need a ride home?"

"No, my Mom is here, and my friend brought me so I'm good but thanks for asking."

Micah startled Saniya as he walked up behind her.

"Hey man, I'm Micah" as he extended his hand to Xavier.

"Hey, I'm Xavier.

"Saniya are you ready?"

"Sure, I'm ready."

"Xavier, I have to go. All I want to do now is go home. Take care."

As they were walking to the car, Micah asked, "Saniya, you okay? You looked a little startled when you saw that guy."

"Yes, I'm just exhausted right now and ready to go." Her Mom was going to stay at the hospital with Shelby and

Lolita until the mortician showed up and she had told Saniya to go home and get some rest. She and Micah left the hospital and when she arrived at home, Micah walked Saniya to the door and gave her a big hug.

"Call me if you need me." Saniya began weeping again.

"This is the worst night ever Micah. My time with you tonight was so fun and now this. My heart just aches right now. Both women who the Lord called home were amazing women and both had poured into me in their own way. They were like grandmothers to me."

Micah pulled Saniya close to him and said, "Saniya, I am so sorry, and she started sobbing into his chest as he held her tight.

"Do you want me to stay here with you until your Mom arrives?"

"That is so sweet of you I will be okay. Thanks so much for everything and I am sorry that you are out so late because of what happened." Saniya give Micah a kiss on the cheek.

"You will never know how much I appreciate you being with me tonight dealing with all of this. Make sure you call me or text me when you get home since it's so late." He gave Saniya a big hug and agreed to do so.

"I will be sure and call and check in on you tomorrow."

As Saniya was crawling into bed, her phone blinked, and she saw that Micha had made it home safely and as she was about to lay down, her phone rang.

"Hello, Saniya. I wanted to make sure that you made it home okay?" It was Xavier. Saniya paused for a moment and then said, "Yes, I made it home okay. I was just getting into bed. I am completely wiped out physically and emotionally right now."

"Well, I just wanted to check on you and tell you that I love you."

Saniya didn't respond but then said, "Good night Xavier, I can't do this right now, as she hung up the phone.

Xavier looked at the phone as a tear ran down his face. He realized now that he had lost the best thing that had happened to him and he wondered if it was too late. He had resolved to get Saniya back, but from the conversation that he just had, he wasn't sure if that was going to happen. He couldn't hang up without telling her that he still loved her.

ISLAND

What's Happening Now?

Island was awakened by his phone ringing early Sunday morning. Island looked at the clock and it was 7 am.

"Who in the world is calling this early? Hello," he answered groggily.

"Mama, calm down, what's wrong? Oh my God! What happened?" Island had sat up in bed listening intently as his mother went on to tell him about Sister Lula and Sister Imogene.

"That is awful, all of this happened yesterday and last night? Wow, I don't know what to say, Mama. Are you okay?" Island could tell that his Mama was shook up by all of this, but she was also strong in her faith. She explained to him that she and Saniya's mama had stayed with Shelby and Lolita until the mortician came and it was extremely late when she got home. She was about to go visit with Sister Lula's family and take them some food and spend some time with them.

"I can't believe that both of them are gone Mama. Wow, it's hard enough when you lose one person, but two in the same day/night; that's unbelievable."

"Well baby, please pray for both families. They are taking it hard because both deaths were unexpected, but we all will have our turn dealing with losing someone close to us." "Mama, I don't want to talk about that now. I can't imagine losing you and I don't even want to think about it."

"Boy, as far as I know I'm not going anywhere yet, but this is a reality that we all must face and deal with. Just know that I love you and remember everything that I have taught you even after I'm gone. That's why it's so important for you to solidify your relationship with the Lord, Island, while you still have time. No one knows when the Lord will call them home. None of it is for us to understand but to make sure that we know the Lord and have a relationship with him. What we do for Him is all that counts. While you are on this earth Island make a difference for the Lord. Remember, the harvest is plentiful, but the workers are few. We have to make a difference while we can. Do you think you will be able to make it back for the funerals?"

"Mama, I will try but it will depend on when they hold the services. Tomorrow is our first day of work in starting to get this office off the ground and up and running. Make sure you let me know when they plan to have the services and I will do all that I can to make sure that I am there even if I have to fly in and back out again in the same day. I will also call the assistant music director to talk to him about the music for the services. Both Sister Lula and Sister Imogene were phenomenal women of God so the music for their homegoing celebrations needs to be uplifting and inspiring."

"You are right Island, there needs to be uplifting music. We must remember that when a saint goes home to be with the Lord, it needs to be a celebration even though our hearts are hurting. You see Island, funerals are for the living because our loved one is meeting face to face with the Lord. Funerals are just a ritual that we started to celebrate the person's life, but you preach your own eulogy while you are living by the way your live your life and treat others." Island thought that his Mama was going to break out shouting and speaking in tongues as she continued to talk to him.

"You're right Mama and I always keep that in mind. With that being said and changing the subject for a moment, I ran into Taylor last night. She is also here in Miami working for the next few months."

"Really?"

"I ran into her at a Cuban restaurant we had dinner at last night. It was kind of awkward, but she looked great. She gave me one of her cards and we hugged."

"Ummm hmmmm." His mom said. "Well, I'm not going to get in your business Island. I have to trust and believe that you will make the right decision and you and Taylor are both adults and know what's best for yourselves." His Mama was dying to ask more questions but she knew better than to get too excited because that would just make Island go the opposite direction. She had learned years ago not to get too involved in Island's personal life. He was so defensive and she didn't want to have an argument or be preaching to him about his life at this moment. She just wanted to let him know what was happening at the home front.

"I will call you back later Island once I find out more about the arrangements. I love you."

"I love you too Mama" and then he hung up. After his call with his Mama, Island couldn't go back to sleep. He realized that he had a dull headache which was probably due to the number of mojitos that he had after seeing Taylor last night.

"Let me get up and get in a workout and then grab some lunch. I will do some work later this evening in preparation for tomorrow." Island went for a run to clear his head. He then came back to his condominium to shower and headed out for lunch.

As he was enjoying his lunch, he heard a familiar voice and when he turned around he saw Carlos and Chandra. "Could this weekend get any crazier than it already has been?" Island thought to himself. First, I run into Taylor, then the deaths at home and now Carlos and Chandra."

"Hey, you guys," Island said as he greeted Carlos and Chandra with a hug.

"What in the world are you doing here in Miami Island?" Chandra asked.

"Well, my company is about to open up a new location here in Miami and my VP asked me to come down here and get the office up and running."

"Really?" Carlos said grinning.

"Yes, I just got here on Thursday night and we start work on tomorrow."

"Well, this calls for a celebration, Island." Island was unsure whether to accept the invitation as he was looking out the side of his eye at Chandra who was looking stunning as ever.

"Well, my schedule is a little crazy right now, Carlos, with this office getting started up," as Island attempted to get out of the invitation.

"Well, you still have to eat Island so why don't we meet later this week, maybe Friday and have dinner. I will call you with the time and location."

"Okay, sounds like fun," Island said hesitantly. "Well, let me keep moving. I have tons to do before getting started tomorrow."

"No, no before you go, we must have a celebratory drink," as Carlos snapped for the waiter.

"Please bring me your best bottle of champagne, we have a toast to make here with our dear friend." The waiter did as he was instructed and returned with a bottle of champagne.

"Here's to old friends and new beginnings Island. Cheers!" They all raised their glasses to each other and sipped the champagne.

"Sweetheart, do you want to make a toast to Island?"

"Sure, here's to new memories," Chandra said. They raised their glasses again.

"Carlos, Chandra, thanks so much but I really have to go and get some work done."

"Okay, Island, since you are going to be a stick in the mud, we will talk later this week."

Island walked off thinking, "I really need to go and pray because he knew that his flesh was getting weak after seeing Taylor and now Carlos and Chandra." Island's mind had started drifting off the last couple of days with snippets of he and Taylor and then he also had thought about the time in Las Vegas with Carlos and Chandra. His mind kept wondering as he was reliving some of the moments of his past, so he knew he needed to get busy with some work. He tried calling Pastor Harris, then Deacon Jones and even Saniya but no one was answering. I just need to sit down and take the edge off. As Island fixed himself another cocktail and flipped the television on there was a love making scene, so he tried turning the channel quickly. It seemed like every channel he turned to it was something that he didn't need to fix his eyes or his mind on at the moment.

"Well, I better go get in the word right now before I give the devil a crack. If I give him a crack in the door, he will kick it in and come in with guns blazing." Little did he know, he was so right.

LOLITA

On My Own

"Aiden, I can't thank you enough for being with me at the hospital the other night. I don't remember a whole lot after Big Mama died but....."

"No problem Lolita. I know what it's like to lose someone you love." There was a moment of silence.

"Well, we just met, and you have already seen me at my worse. I'm a true southern girl so I try to always look my best and I will say that this week has not been my finest moment."

"Nobody expects you to be dolled up and looking gorgeous while you are grieving Lolita. Don't even think like that. It's not about that." About that time, Lolita heard the doorbell.

"Aiden, can you hold for a moment? There's someone at the door." As Lolita opened the door, there was a delivery guy with a beautiful bouquet of flowers.

"I have a delivery for Lolita Johnson."

"I'm Lolita Johnson."

"Please sign here." The bouquet was so big that Lolita ask the delivery guy to bring them into the parlor and place them on the table. "Thank you so much." She opened the card and read it. "Lolita, I am sorry for your loss. I hope these flowers help to brighten your day just a little bit." – Aiden.

When Lolita picked up the phone she said, "Aiden, you shouldn't have."

"I shouldn't have what?"

"I just received the most beautiful bouquet from you."

"Well, I wanted to try and bring you a little bit of sunshine right now. I hope that they made you smile."

"Yes, they did, and I can't thank you enough."

"Once your grandmother's services have taken place and things have settled down, I would like to take you to dinner and hopefully then we will concentrate on getting to know each other a little bit more. It just seems like now is not the appropriate time for me to be trying to ask you out on a date with you just losing your grandmother."

"Aiden, you are so sweet," Lolita said.

"Beautiful flowers for a beautiful lady. Please let me know about the services and if there is anything that I can do for you, please don't hesitate to let me know."

"Thanks again Aiden. I will keep that in mind. Goodbye."

As Lolita hung up the phone and sat down, she realized that this was the first time in her life that she didn't have a man to comfort her during a trying time and now look here is this new man that is interested in her but is he too good to be true she thought to herself. All she could think about was the song by Patti LaBelle and Michael McDonald – On My Own.

"Why, I need to stop thinking this way. My therapist has told me only positive thoughts. Why shouldn't I have a nice man like Aiden interested in me? He seems sincere and he is already in the Lord so it's not somebody that I have to drag into a relationship with the Lord." Lolita and her assistant had done some snooping after Aiden and his sister had left her boutique. She found out that he came from a very well to do family. His father was a judge and his mother had been a corporate executive. He owned several different businesses, a couple of hotels, a bed and breakfast and even had an accounting firm so he was set financially. The only thing that she didn't know was whether he had been married or had children; not much about his private life was online.

"I guess I will have to wait to find out more about him. Now I need to concentrate on getting Big Mama's services done." About that time here doorbell rang. It was Shelby. Lolita could tell that she had been crying just like her and when their eyes met they embraced each other and cried some more.

"Lolita, I just can't believe that Big Mama is gone."

"I know, I can't believe it either. Neither one of us saw this coming because Big Mama was so self-sufficient and able to do for herself. It all seems so surreal."

"We just didn't realize that it would come so fast and so soon. We have spent so much time hating each other the last year or so and trying to stay out of each other's way that we didn't realize that our strained relationship was probably taking a toll on Big Mama as well. You know Lolita, we have had some major mess going on over the last two years, but we are still sisters and I want to salvage as much of our relationship as possible."

"Likewise, Shelby. I no longer hate you and blame you for what happened between Rashad and me. I have learned to accept my responsibility in all the stuff between Rashad and me and like Big Mama asked us to forgive each other, I do forgive you and I still love you because you're my sister. I honestly don't know that our relationship will ever be the same. Only God can fix what is broken and repair it like brand new." There was a moment of silence.

"I saw that Rashad brought you to the hospital the other night when everything happened. Are you two together now?"

Shelby hesitated and then said, "Rashad has given me an ultimatum and told me that he will not continue waiting for me forever."

"Well, I understand that Shelby. You couldn't wait to have him and now that you can have him, it appears that you don't want him."

"That's not it!" Shelby exclaimed.

"Well, you could have fooled me. After Rashad and I got divorced, I just knew you would have leaped at your chance to have him all to yourself, but now you are hesitant."

"It's because of my children, Lolita, along with James threatening me," Shelby said softly.

"Shelby, you are a lot of things, but a bad mother is not one of them. We have raised our children together and I'm sure if you sit down and talk with James and stop letting him make demands on you that you both can come to an agreement. I don't agree with how you go about getting what you want Shelby, but I will make sure and do everything that I can to help you not lose your children. You may be a ...." and Lolita caught herself mid-sentence and simply stated, "You don't deserve to lose your children because you made a mistake. I think that James has calmed down by now and he should know that a judge will not take your children away from you because of your mistake. I truly believe that he was hurt just like I was and taking it out on you and the only way he could really hurt you was threatening to take your children from you."

"I hope you are right because I have repented to God and I have decided to stop living in fear and ask James for a divorce after all of this is over with, but right now, I just want us to make it through all of this in one piece."

DEACON JONES

What Next?

As Deacon Jones waited for the prayer group to arrive at his home, his heart was heavy. "Lord, what do I do now? This was a week that I was not prepared for and it has been devastating to me." About the time, Deacon Jones got caught up in his thoughts, the doorbell rang.

"Hello Deacon," Pastor Harris exclaimed.

"Hello Pastor. Come on in. I was just sitting here reflecting on the past week and waiting for the prayer group to arrive. The services this week were beautiful. You really helped us to focus on the good times with Sister Imogene and with Sister Lula. Both of those ladies made a tremendous impact on so many members of our congregation both young and old. Both funerals were standing room only which tells me how much both ladies were loved and admired by everyone," Deacon said as he went to answer the door again. One by one the prayer group arrived and then Deacon continued his conversation with Pastor Harris.

"Deacon, I know this week has been hard for you. How are you doing with all of this?"

"Yes, all is well. I'm just still trying to digest everything that has happened over this past week. Two of my friends are no longer here."

"These young people don't understand what it's like to grow old and then you start losing family members and then your friends and pretty soon you look around and everybody is gone. I guess that's why the Lord says in his word that this is not our home and we are just traveling through here." *1 Chronicles 29:15.*

"You're right, Deacon. After a while, we start having a yearning to be with the Lord and not be here on earth because this isn't our home. Once we come to understand that and know that you will be with Him and be able to see your loved ones again, things start coming into perspective. It's not to say that it makes it any easier because we still feel the pain of losing our loved ones, but we know we will see them again," Pastor Harris said.

"Island, I am happy that you were able to be in town for the services."

"I wouldn't have missed either of them and I am thankful that you had both of them back to back so that I could attend. I am catching a flight back to Miami in a few hours. I hope both families enjoyed the praise and worship music that we had for the services. I wanted to keep it uplifting since both ladies loved the Lord and loved on all of us with all our issues. All of the stories that people shared made me realize even more how special both were." The prayer group shared stories with one another and told how much Sister

Lula and Sister Imogene had impacted their lives. It was a joyous and sad occasion for all of them.

"Well Deacon, we better get out of here and let you get some rest. Thank you for having this little gathering for the prayer group to come together and share our memories."

"No problem, glad to do it."

As Deacon Jones said goodbye to everyone and threw away some trash, he just started sobbing uncontrollably.

"Lord, why? I can't believe my friends are gone. I was starting to fall in love with Lula even though she was older than me. We were having a blast with one another. I don't understand why you keep taking people that I love!" Deacon Jones shouted. Of course, there was silence in the room except for his conversation with the Lord.

"Is this what you are doing to punish me for all of my years of bad behavior? I have repented from all of that foolishness and you still punish me." *Your sins are as far as the east is from the west and I remember them no more – Psalm 103:12.* He heard in his spirit.

"It sure feels like I am being punished!" But the Deacon knew better. He had read that God only wants what's best for us. He was just lashing out in anger, hurt and frustration like so many people do when they are grieving, they lash out at God and blame Him.

"If I'm going to be in this much pain then I need something to help me deal with it," he thought to himself. I don't want to have this much pain in my life, it's not fair." He thought about having a drink and about that time,

Deacon Jones phone rang, and it was one of his old running buddies.

"Hey man, I just wanted to check and see if you wanted to hang out with me and the fellas for a little while tonight? We promise we won't keep you out late."

Deacon Jones sat there for a minute and then said, "What the hell?" He hung up and let his pain take him out the door and back into the streets. He wanted something familiar and he was on his way to what he had known for years before truly knowing the Lord.

In the spiritual realm, the enemy was talking out loud to himself. I knew that I could get him to revert to his old ways. God thought he had him but now look. He has forgotten all about God and turned back to his old ways as the enemy laughed. This is going to be a fun season for me. I am the puppet master and I will make him do whatever I want. I will make all of this little group bend to my ways."

SANIYA

Torn Between Two Loves

Saniya thought she was dreaming when she heard her phone, but it was her phone ringing.

"Hello?" Saniya answered groggily.

"Good morning beautiful" and Saniya instantly started smiling. It was Micah on the other end.

"Good morning, Sir," Saniya said smiling to herself.

"How are you this morning?" he asked.

"I'm better but I didn't realize that it's almost 10 am. I don't normally sleep this late, but I guess that I was wiped out by being up so late this week."

"Yes, you probably needed the rest. I just wanted to let you know regardless of all that has taken place this week, I did have a nice night out with you and I had been praying for you and your church family and friends this week."

"You are so sweet Micah and I truly appreciate you taking me to the hospital and bringing me home the other night. Most of the people you saw at the hospital were family members of Sister Imogene's and the folks from our prayer group that I told you about. By the way, I want to be up front with you as she paused for a moment. Xavier and I used to date and broke up last year. I was shocked to see him the other night, but I was glad that he was there for the families involved."

"Well, I saw him hug you, but I didn't want to assume anything and that was none of my business. I know that you know a lot of people and I'm sure a lot of people hug you. I'm not that insecure and I realize that you have had a life prior to meeting me."

"Wow, you are beyond your years Mr. Micah. If it had been the other way around, Xavier would have played twenty questions with me and being asking who you were, how I knew you, etc."

"Look Saniya, I'm like you and don't like playing games with people and their emotions so as long as we stay up front and honest with one another, we should be good. I really want to get to know you better and take things slow. That is, if you are interested? I don't want us rushing into anything because I am serious about getting my career started and I also want to be married and one day start a family, but Lord knows I want to do everything the right way. I have had my heart broken and it's no fun, so I totally get where you are right now. For all I know, you may still have feelings for Xavier and if that's the case, I would understand. I want to know that if we continue to move forward being friends and seeing where this goes, I want to know that you are fully committed and over Xavier. One of the things that I have learned is not to jump from relationship to relationship. We need to learn who we are and what we really want out of a relationship and out of life. We don't want to tote the baggage we accumulated in one relationship into another one and that's what happens when we jump around from one person to another. For example, you may still have a distrust of men because of what happened in your relationship with Xavier." Saniya agreed with him and said that she had come to terms that she did have some trust issues, but her Mom had talked to her about that.

"My Mom told me that I can't blame all men for my bad choice. There were signs there but when we started sleeping together, I didn't pay attention to those signs because my head was all foggy because of the sex."

"Your Mom is right on that one, plus we often confuse lust with love. We know that having a physical attraction is important and the intimacy in a relationship is important but that can't be the foundation of your relationship because it will be superficial. Saniya, I want you to be my best friend more than anything before we ever take it a step further. I want to make sure that Xavier is completely out of your system."

"Is this dude for real?" Saniya was thinking to herself.

As Saniya was laying in her bed continuing to talk to Micah, she realized he was so much more mature than she was about a lot of things. She listened to him as he continued to talk, and they continued to laugh and cut up, but in the back of her mind, she began to wonder whether she was over Xavier. Her mind drifted to thoughts of making love with Xavier and she heard Micah calling her name.

"I'm sorry Micah, I must still be tired," she said quickly.

"Well, I'm going to let you go so you can continue resting. Just buzz me later if that's okay."

"Sure, it is and I look forward to seeing you again," as she smiled.

Saniya tried to go back to sleep, she heard her phone ping and saw that Micah had sent her a cute message. She smiled and thought to herself, "Am I really over Xavier? Micah is a nice guy and I am enjoying spending time with him but he's not Xavier. He's almost too good to be true.

In the spiritual realm, the enemy laughed to himself as he started to implement his plan to make Saniya have second thoughts about Micah. He whispered, "That's right Saniya, you like that bad boy image and roughness about Xavier. Micah talks about God all the time, he may be too boring for you. You need someone like Xavier who can love you the way you need to be loved."

About that time, Saniya heard the doorbell ring. Saniya yelled, "Mom, can you get the door?" There was no answer, so Saniya grabbed her robe and ran downstairs. "Mom must have left to run errands," Saniya said to herself. When she opened the door, there was a bouquet of roses on the front porch and she saw the flower delivery truck driving away.

"What in the world?" As she picked up the bouquet and went back inside, she pulled out the card. "Beautiful flowers for a beautiful woman who still has my heart" and it was signed – With all my love – X. Saniya felt as if she was about to stop breathing.

ISLAND

Unexpected Moments

"What a week and now it's already the weekend. Is my time in Miami going to fly by like this week flew by?" Island wondered. "The first week is done, I have seen Taylor, Carlos and Chandra and attended two funerals back to back. Boy, I am exhausted. I am also starving, and I haven't even gone to the grocery store, so I guess I will be ordering in or going out to eat."

With all the good food in Miami, Island didn't mind going out to eat especially since his meals and food would be covered by the firm. "Let me see what I'm in the mood for tonight," he said as he flipped through menus that had been left in his condominium. About that time, his phone rang. It was a number that he didn't recognize but he answered anyway.

"Hello?"

"Hey Island, it's Taylor, how are you?"

"I'm okay, just trying to decide what I want to have for dinner. It has been a crazy first week."

"Well, I wanted to see if you were available for dinner tomorrow night?"

"Oh," Island said unsuspectingly. Well, I would love to have dinner with you tomorrow night Taylor."

"Okay, I will text you the time and details. We have a lot of catching up to do."

"Yes, we do."

"I will see you tomorrow night then," Taylor said and hung up the phone. He wasn't sure what to make of the phone call. He thought that Taylor may still be angry and upset with him, but it is sounding like she has gotten over everything that happened between them. Either she had gotten over everything or she was going to kill him. Island knew that he had hurt Taylor terribly and always wanted to make sure that she knew that none of what happened was her fault. He still wanted to apologize even more to her and make sure that she had forgiven him for hurting her so bad.

"Maybe this can be a fresh start for us and maybe we can still be friends. Who knows what the future brings?" More than ten minutes later, Island's phone rang again. It was another number that he didn't recognize but decided to answer because it was a local number.

"Hello, my friend, how are you?" Island recognized the voice. It was Carlos.

"Hey man, what's going on?"

"Nothing much. I told you I would let you get through your first week and then we need to get together for dinner, so what about tonight or tomorrow night?"

"I already have plans for tomorrow night with an old friend, but I'm free tonight or Sunday night."

"Why don't we shoot for an early dinner on Sunday

night. I will send you the address and the time and we will see you then."

"Okay Carlos sounds like a plan" and then Island said goodbye.

"Well, maybe I should order in tonight and get to bed early since I have two dinner invitations for the weekend." Island continued looking through the menus, placed an order for delivery and decided to relax until his food arrived. He ate dinner and watched television and then decided to have a massage therapist come to his room to give him a massage. As he was receiving his massage, he let his mind drift back to how much fun he and Taylor used to have and then on to his flings with other men. Island wanted to be able to block out all the visions in his mind of the men that he had been with, but for some reason they continued to pop up. Pastor Harris and Deacon Jones had told him that when he has those images pop up in his mind that he needs to picture Jesus on the cross. He tried that and sometimes it worked and sometimes it didn't work. One thing was that Island wasn't fully ready to let go of his lifestyle. He liked what he liked, and he realized that women didn't turn him on the way other men did; not even Taylor. Deep down he loved Taylor, but did he love her enough to change? There had been a lot of men and women coming out of the closet lately about their lifestyle and there were states that were even considering letting same sex couples marry, but Island wasn't sure he was ready for all of that. Something in him just wouldn't let him come out and tell everybody that he was homosexual or bisexual. He wasn't even sure how to define himself. He enjoyed the time that he had with Taylor, but he found his escapades with other men more exciting. Here he was again in a state of confusion about his life.

"Maybe I should just pretend like I was doing before. I can marry Taylor and just try and concentrate on being a good husband to her and we can start a family. What if that doesn't do it for me, then I am back at square one and hurting her again?"

"Mr. Island, I am finished."

"Oh, I'm sorry Tina. I dosed off for a few minutes and didn't realize that you had stopped massaging me. Thanks so much. I needed that." Island put on his robe and paid Tina and she left.

"Now I am going to sit here and have me a glass of wine and lay in my bed and watch some television." As Island began to relax and watch a movie, his mind still wandered to Taylor and then back to Carlos. He started to feel his flesh rise and thought to himself that it had been weeks or maybe months before he had the kind of release that he really wanted to have. His doorbell rang so he grabbed his robe and put it back on and when he opened the door, Carlos was standing in front of him.

"I couldn't wait to see you on Sunday," as Carlos slammed the door and grabbed him and kissed him. Island wanted to resist but at the same time was just thinking about this very thing happening. Everything that he had been daydreaming about in fulfilling his flesh was now coming true and he hadn't even asked for it. This was a moment of hot, steamy passion like he had when he was in

Las Vegas. He wanted badly to tell Carlos to stop but he couldn't make the words form and come out of his mouth.

Island thought, "I have been depriving myself for months so why not?" He gave in to his flesh and let Carlos fulfill his fantasy although this time Chandra was not involved. Before Island knew it, it was morning and the sun was coming up. As he rolled over, he realized that Carlos must have left sometime during the night or early morning and here he was feeling empty inside again.

In the spiritual realm, the enemy was laughing to himself again.

"I'm taking out this little prayer group one by one and it's not even as hard as I thought it would be. They love having their flesh fulfilled and I can just keep giving them what they want and see if they don't turn their backs on their God."

LOLITA

I Still Got It

Lolita was glad that the week was over and that Big Mama's service was over and done with.

"I just need to rest some for the next couple of days and then Shelby and I need to make sure we have all of Big Mama's affairs in order. We need to stop her social security, we need to close out her account at the bank and we need to make a decision about the house and her car." Lolita had decided to make a list of things to do and then call Shelby so that they could decide to work together or take the list and work separately. Lolita heard her phone ringing and was trying to dig it out of her purse before it went to voice mail.

"Hello," she said.

"Good morning beautiful lady how are you today?" It was Aiden and the minute Lolita heard his voice she got a big smile on her face. Aiden was like a breath of fresh air to her.

"I'm doing good and yourself?"

"I can't complain. I just wanted to check in on you to see how you were faring this week after everything that has taken place."

"I'm making it okay. I have my moments where

everything seems so surreal and then I realize all of this did happen. It hurts, but I am going to take it one day at a time, that's all that I can do."

"Yes, I understand exactly what you mean. I haven't shared this with you Lolita, but I am going to share it with you now. Life can throw us some fast pitches that we are not ready for, but we learn to swing at them and move on. When my wife and my son died, I thought that my world would come to an end." Lolita gasped.

"Aiden, I am so sorry."

"No, don't be, it was years ago. I know what heartbreak feels like and I know what it's like to have unsurmountable grief. I didn't even want to live, but I had to learn to live without them. There's not a day that goes by that I don't think of them, but life continues to go on and I continue to learn how to live my life without them. I just started getting out more this past year and learning that living is not so bad after all. God has constantly assured me that He is with me through it all. He will also be with you and your sister Lolita as well. I am here for you if you ever need to talk or if you just need a shoulder to cry on. That's what I can do for you. Grief is an unusual thing Lolita and it can take over you if you let it. The thing is that you kind of have to go with the flow of it. When you feel like crying, cry, when you need to lie down for a bit lie down but just don't stay down. Learn how to reflect on the good times and the memories that you have made with your grandmother. It's obvious that she was very important in your life and helped shape you into the woman you are today."

As Lolita's eyes watered up she said, "Thanks so much Aiden for your kind words. The last couple of years have been a rollercoaster for my sister and me. We had a period where we stopped speaking because we were so angry with one another. If it hadn't been for my grandmother and our prayer group, we probably wouldn't be speaking or talking to each other today. Since we are sharing, I feel the need to tell you why my sister and I were at odds. My sister, Shelby, had an affair with my husband which is what lead to us finally divorcing. Don't get me wrong, our marriage had been in trouble for some time, but after learning the truth of him and my sister, that was more than I could take. I had my share in making the marriage a disaster as well, so it was not all his fault. I have learned a lot about myself over the last year while I was in therapy and I feel like my life is just beginning again."

"I'm glad to hear that you're in therapy to help you with all of this. Far too often, we as African Americans refuse to seek out professional counseling even when we know we need some help coping with life. I know it worked wonders for me and I don't mind telling folks to get whatever help you need to get you through whatever you are going through. Some Jesus and some counseling does a body and mind good."

"Well, it sounds like we have a lot to share with one another Lolita, but I do believe that the best is yet to come for both of us. Just let me know when you are available again. I would love to take you on a real date where we can sit down and start getting to know one another. Does that sound like a plan to you?"

"Yes, Aiden it sounds like a plan to me," she said smiling to herself.

"Well, you have a blessed day Lolita and I hope to hear from you soon. Goodbye."

Lolita was beginning to like all this attention she was getting from Aiden. She glanced at herself in the mirror and said, "not bad girlfriend – you still got it." It was nice to have a man pay attention to her and not want something in return. She always felt as if her marriage with Rashad was give, give and give some more. She poured everything into him and their daughter and really didn't concentrate on herself.

"It's my turn now to be happy and to do what I want to do without feeling guilty about it. I deserve to be happy just like everyone else and I have learned that another human being can't give you happiness, you have to already have it. Lord, I thank you for the lessons that you have taught me over the last year. They have been painful but because of that pain, I won't ever forget them. God has shown me that there is purpose in my pain. I have learned not to ever put a man on a pedestal but to always have you first and foremost. I have learned that I deserve the best and I deserve to be loved like a woman should be loved. Rashad took me for granted for far too long and I let him get away with so much stuff longer than I should have. Lord, please forgive me for losing myself and taking my focus from you – that was the biggest mistake of my life. Lord, I ask that you continue to lead me and guide me in the direction that you would have for me to go and I'm going to listen to you this time and not compare myself with my sister. She has her own demons to fight." As Lolita stopped talking to the Lord, she sat down just to have some peace and quiet with the Lord and meditate on all that had happened to her over the last year or two. She had learned that she needed to be still for the Lord to speak for her so that's why she enjoyed her quiet moments early in the morning with the Lord to get her day started right.

SHELBY

He's Still the One

As Shelby soaked in her bathtub, she thought about all the events that had taken place this past year. She thought about her relationship with James and her relationship with Rashad. She loved Rashad with every fiber of her being and had loved him for some time. She didn't want to miss the opportunity of being with him again for fear that it would be the last chance for them. Shelby thought about the conversations that she had with Big Mama and with Sister Lula. Some of the things resonated within her and for once in her life she had the chance to be with Rashad and she was letting fear control her. She knew how much she loved her children and how much she had loved James. They were just not the same people that they were years ago.

"Sure, all of this is messy, but I am tired of living like a prisoner and if Rashad wants to be with me and has been willing to wait this long, why should I keep him waiting?"

She also thought about what Lolita had said to her that she had waited all this time to get Rashad and now that she had the opportunity she was running scared. Shelby realized that she had not ever backed down from anything and she usually went after whatever she wanted so why should this be any different? She knew she was a good mother and with Lolita on her side vouching for her, she would be a fierce competitor in court if James decided to take that route. She had decided that she was going to sit down and talk to James and her children tonight about her decision. About that time, Shelby's phone startled her thoughts. She decided not to rush out of the tub but to let the call go to the answering machine. She soaked in the tub a little bit longer and then got out and checked her phone. It was a beautiful message from Rashad calling to check in on her and telling her that he loved her. Shelby thought to herself, "After all these years we still have it for one another – that amazes me." Then as she was listening to his message again her phone beeped with another call and a number she didn't recognize so she sent it to her voicemail. She decided to go pick up the children so that she could have a conversation with them alone and then she would talk to James tonight over dinner or after dinner. She was feeling nervous about how he would react to her since he was acting warden in the house and they hadn't had a pleasant moment since he found out about the affair. She had asked him how long he was going to punish her for her mistake and he would just look at her with disgust and walk off.

"He has grounds biblically to divorce me, but he would rather make my life miserable instead. Who does that? I know that I hurt him badly, but I shouldn't have to pay for this mistake the rest of my life and live with the threat of him taking my children away from me. I am not a bad mother and I love my children." Shelby could feel her blood pressure rising as she thought about how James had been treating her. She decided that she was going to be civil with him and not be a "b" with him when they talked even if he talked crazy to her. Big Mama had taught them that someone always has to remain calm even though she and Lolita had not acted accordingly last year. They learned to deal with one another as adults.

Later that evening Shelby told her children they were going to go out and have dinner. They asked if James was coming with them and Shelby told them no, it would just be the three of them. They seemed somewhat overjoyed at the thought of having some quality time alone with their mother. When they got to the restaurant and had dinner, everyone seemed to be having a good time.

"Kids, as you know things have been kind of tense in our house for a while now with me and your Daddy. I want to apologize for how we have behaved at times in front of you and I want you to both know that your Daddy and I love you very much."

"Mama, we know that you and Daddy love us. You tell us all the time and we know that things have been weird with the two of you, but we just figured it was grown-up stuff."

Shelby smiled a little and replied, "Yes it was grown up stuff. Sometimes, we as grown-ups don't always act like grown-ups but more like children. I want you to know that anything that happens between me and your Daddy has nothing to do with the two of you."

"Mama, what are you getting to?" her youngest and spunkiest asked her.

"Well, your Daddy and I have not been happy with each other for some time and right now we seem to be making each other miserable. Mama did something that hurt your Daddy very much and I have apologized and asked him to accept my apology and forgive me, but he is having a really hard time doing so."

"Are you and Daddy going to get divorced like Aunt Lolita and Uncle Rashad?" The question caught Shelby off guard, but she responded.

"Right now, I'm not exactly sure about what your Daddy and I are going to do. I will be talking to him tonight but regardless of what happens, we both love you and we will always love you."

"Lexie gets to spend time with her Mama and also with her Daddy and he takes her to do fun stuff all the time since he and Aunt Lolita don't live together anymore."

"So, you see, even though Aunt Lolita and Uncle Rashad are no longer together they both still get to spend quality time with Lexi. Sometimes grown-ups grow apart and seek out different things when they aren't happy with one another."

Her children kind of looked at her with a puzzled look. "Well, I just wanted to spend some time with you and talk to you guys before I talked to Daddy."

"Mama, we want you and Daddy to be happy and not make each other mad and miserable all the time. We have a lot of friends whose parents are divorced, and they live with both of them off and on. Their parents have a visitation schedule. If you and Daddy don't live together, who would we live with?"

"Well, I would hope that you would want to live with me, and your Daddy and I could work out a schedule so that you could see him whenever you wanted to as well. I still have some things to work out and to discuss with your Daddy but either way we will sit down and talk to you both once we make some decisions. Okay?"

"Okay, now can we go for ice cream too?"

"Sure, we can." Shelby felt somewhat relieved but at the same time saddened that it didn't seem like a big deal to her children and that they had already realized on their own that things were different between her and James. It made her sad that her babies had already been exposed to divorce and it was becoming the norm for them and their friends.

"Was this the new normal in our society? Maybe there are a lot of people that figure out later in life that they have married the wrong person. Did we mess it up? Did we get off course from what God has for us in the first place or are we just fulfilling our own desires now?" Shelby had so many questions running through her mind that she was like the kids and wanted to have some ice cream to take her mind off things and her dreaded conversation with James.

Later that night after the children were asleep, Shelby went downstairs to the master bedroom located on the main floor to talk to James. She had been thankful over the last year that they had a home with an upstairs master and a downstairs master bedroom so that she and James could go to their respective corners after they battled. Shelby knocked on the door and James opened it.

"Oh, I thought you were one of the kids."

"No, it's just me. I wanted to know if we could sit down and talk with one another like two adults and not yell and scream?"

"Sure, come on in."

"James, I keep apologizing to you for all of the mess that I have caused, and you keep treating me like a dog. I have apologized and asked for your forgiveness and you are still so angry with me. I don't know what else to do but I know that I will not continue the rest of my life being miserable." There was a long pause and James just looked at her.

"What are you trying to say Shelby?"

Shelby swallowed hard and then said, "I want a divorce."

James looked at her and then handed her a brown envelope.

"What is this?"

"I'm giving you what you want Shelby. I have loved you the best way that I know how over the years. I have provided for you, let you do whatever you wanted to, and it never seems to be enough. Sure, I haven't been a perfect husband sometimes concentrating more on work than I should but that was to provide the best for you and the kids, so I didn't mind. Over this past year, I have done a lot of thinking myself and asking myself a lot of questions. Did you love me when you married me? Were you still in love with Rashad? How did we get to this point Shelby?"

By this time, Shelby had tears in her eyes and she said,

"James I did love you when we met and got married but I don't think that I ever really got over Rashad. He had been my first love and when things went south with him, I just jumped back into another relationship and that was with you. I don't have any regrets about marrying you, but I feel like I should have let my heart heal first before moving on or at least had some closure on my relationship with him, but I was so hurt when he married my sister that I just kept it moving. We don't realize the baggage that we bring into relationships until later in life when we sit down, hold the mirror up to our face and ask ourselves some serious questions. I am truly sorry for what I did to us James. At first, I thought we should go to counseling and try and save our marriage especially after you threatened to take our children from me. After you refused counseling and treated me so bad, I knew this was not going to end like a fairy tale and even if it did and we decided to stay together we are still back at square one. I would still have feelings for Rashad and you would wonder if I truly loved you. None of that is fair to you. James, you have been a great husband and I really didn't deserve you. I don't want us to hate one another. We have built a beautiful life together over the years and have two beautiful children together. We have some great memories together, but I don't want them destroyed because I have been selfish. I can't tell you how many times I cried after seeing Rashad because I wanted so badly to be with him but at the same time, I wanted to be with you."

"Shelby is it that you loved me and wanted to be with me

or was it that you loved the lifestyle that I have provided for you?"

Shelby looked up and said, "It was,,," and James put his hand up to stop her from saying anything.

"Never mind, I think I already know the answer to the question. Shelby, I really hope that you find whatever makes you happy. If I don't then why should I hold you hostage here by forcing you to stay with me if you don't love me?"

"James, I do love you, but I still feel like something is missing in my life."

"Well, I hope you find it Shelby and that you don't do anymore damage along the way. Review the paperwork and let me know if you are agreeable to the terms that I had the attorney draft up and we can talk again later. My only regret Shelby is that our kids got caught in our cross fire and they don't deserve this. At the same time, I don't want them staying in a house that isn't a home for them so if that means going our separate ways and co-parenting, then so be it. I am sorry that I have treated you so bad over this past year, but I was really hurt by everything and my ego was hurt so I lashed out at you. I should have never threatened to take our children away from you. I was only trying to hurt you like you had hurt me."

"James, I am so sorry" and she reached for his hand and hugged him and they both cried and held onto one another. As Shelby left the room, she was truly sorry about how badly she had hurt James. Her marriage was ending in divorce and at the same time she wondered if she was making a mistake leaving him for Rashad. This was the third death she was experiencing in a short time period. The death of a marriage is just like losing someone to death itself. You have all kinds of memories both good and bad and then they all come to a halt and sometimes you're ready and sometimes you're not.

DEACON JONES

The day after

As Deacon Jones rolled over in his bed, his head felt like someone had bashed him in the back of his head with a brick. He could barely raise his head off the pillow and then he remembered this old familiar feeling, it was a hangover. Deacon hadn't drank since Mona died and now here he was with a hangover.

"What in the world was I thinking last night going out with my old friends? Nothing good could have come from me going back out in those streets, but why should I sit here and be miserable. Lord, every time I find happiness with someone, you seem to rip my heart out again and again. I know you hear me talking to you but now you are all quiet. Why didn't you stop me from going out last night? Surely, you knew what the outcome would be." All Deacon remembered was ordering one drink and then another and another. He was reminiscing with all his old buddies and they were catching up on old times and all that had taken place since Mona died. His friends said that they had missed him and missed hanging out with him over the last year or so and it seemed like old times. He didn't even remember how he got home last night but he looked outside and saw his car parked crooked. He knew that he had driven home drunk.

"Oh, my goodness, I can't believe that I got behind the wheel of a car drunk again." As Deacon was preparing himself something to drink and grabbing some Tylenol, he thought about what lead him to the events of last night – pain.

"I have got to find a better way to deal with pain, but I have been dealing with it the only way I know how just like my Daddy dealt with everything with a drink. I had made it over a year without a drink and now I feel as if I have to start all over again with my sobriety."

The Holy Spirit reminded him that he was a new creation and that old things had passed away.

"If old things have passed away then why am I still tempted to drink?"

"That was a choice that you made Deacon. I didn't make it, you did and your hangover is the result of your bad choice you made last night. You haven't had a drink in over a year until last night. Remember, I will never leave you or forsake you. You could have turned to me but instead you choose to drink and hang with your buddies. Where were your buddies when Mona died? Were they there for you? They are still doing the same thing that they have always done and you made a change in your life and decided to seek out me after something horrible happened to you. Have your buddies been supportive of you and your walk with me? Did they come to service with you after everything had happened when you gave your testimony? Have they been there for you over the

last year when you were feeling alone and helpless without Mona?
Were they there to support you when I called Lula home? You
keep letting your "friends" lead you away from me. Remember a
companion of fools will be destroyed (Proverbs 13:20). Not the fool
but the companion of fools. Don't you realize the enemy's goal is
to steal, kill and destroy (John 10:10)? He will run rampant in your
life if you let him, but you have the power to stop him. About
that time, the phone rang and Deacon thought his head
was going to explode so he sent the call to voice mail and
went back to bed. A couple of minutes later, his phone rang
again, and he sent that call to voice mail as well.

Pastor Harris hung up the phone after leaving a message
for Deacon Jones. Deacon had been on his heart a lot lately
and he decided to call and check in on him to see how
he was doing after Lula and Imogene. He knew that he as
having a hard time with all that had happened, and he was
praying that Deacon would stay strong. He also knew that
the flesh was a powerful thing along with our emotions.

Marcus had also been calling his Dad. He hung up after
leaving a message for his Dad. He knew that he was
struggling with losing his friends and he just wanted to
make sure he was okay.

"Honey, I am going by my Dad's house because he's not
answering the phone and hasn't returned any of my calls
and I'm starting to worry about him."

"Okay, sounds like you should do that especially after the
last couple of weeks that he has had. He may be having a
hard time and feeling overwhelmed with all of this. I will see
you later, go spend some time with him that would probably

make him feel better." Marcus hugged and kissed his wife and then headed to his Dad's house.

When Marcus got to Deacon's house, he saw how his Dad's car was parked and he really started to worry. Marcus banged on his door and no one answered so Marcus used his spare key to go into the house.

"Dad, Dad!"

No response. So, Marcus went to his parent's bedroom and found his Dad fast asleep. He saw his clothes on the floor. They reeked of alcohol and cigarette smoke. Marcus gathered up his clothes and took them to the laundry room and then he sat down in the recliner and started to pray for his father. He was afraid that this would happen, that his Dad would backslide and go back to his old ways, so he decided to stay there until his Dad woke up. As Marcus looked around the home that his parents had built, he thought about the good times and the bad times and the times that his Mama had prayed at night for Deacon to return home safely after a night on the town with his boys. He remembered seeing his Mama on her knees praying all the time and now Deacon had finally surrendered to Christ only to go back out in the streets. Marcus could feel his blood pressure rising as he thought about his Mama and how she had died and he decided to pray some more so that he could talk calmly to his Dad when he woke up.

As Marcus sat waiting, he decided to check his Dad's mail. He found what looked like an invitation. He didn't open it but put it on top of his mail. "Maybe, it will be something positive for him to get him out of the house and to have some good clean fun." He collected all the junk mail and disposed of it. He then checked to make sure that his Dad didn't have any past due notices. He didn't so he appeared to be handling his business. Even though his Dad had stayed in the streets, they never worried about bills not being paid. Marcus decided to sit down now and wait for his Dad to wake up. He needed the Holy Spirit to guide him in this conversation and to remove himself and his flesh.

SANIYA

Life Lessons — Truth and Pain

As Saniya picked up her phone, she hesitated. She wanted to call Xavier and thank him for the beautiful flowers but part of her didn't want to do so. She would be fine if she didn't think about Xavier and didn't see him or talk to him but once she heard his voice or smelled his cologne all those memories would start rushing back.

"I hate not to call that would be rude if I didn't thank him for the flowers," so she decided to do so.

"Hello?"

"Hello Xavier, it's Saniya."

"Hey you."

"Hey," Saniya said. "I just wanted to call you and thank you for the beautiful bouquet of flowers. I was surprised and they made my day."

"You are more than welcome. I wanted to surprise you and make you smile after the crazy week we have all had."

"Well, you succeeded." There was a moment of silence.

"Saniya, I don't want you to think that I'm being pushy but can I take you to dinner tomorrow night?"

"I, I don't know if that's such a good idea Xavier."

"Come on Saniya, I just want to see you and talk to you. Baby, I miss you so much and I have realized that I made a huge mistake so please just let me do this one thing, please."

"Let me think about it and I will get back to you later on today."

"Okay, I will be waiting to hear from you and don't have me waiting all day, girl."

"Seriously? Did you just?" Xavier cut her off.

"Saniya, I was just joking. See you are always trippin out," he laughed.

"I may give you an answer and I may not after that." They both laughed and said goodbye.

Saniya wanted to talk to her mother about this situation but she already knew that her mother was going to tell her to keep it moving with Micah and forget about Xavier. About that time Saniya heard her mom come in through the garage and go into the kitchen.

"Saniya!" her mom yelled.

"Yes ma'am."

"Where did these flowers come from? Never mind, I see the card." Saniya forgot to bring the flowers upstairs and put them in her room. She wasn't ready to have this conversation with her Mom but she may as well be because she could hear her Mom coming up the stairs.

"Hey Mama."

"Hey you. How are you today?"

"I'm good. I think I'm just tired from all that has been going on this week.

As Saniya's Mom sat down on the bed, Saniya knew this was one of their Mother-Daughter moments.

"Well, I see Mr. Xavier has surfaced again. I saw him at the hospital the other night and I was glad that he was there to support everybody but I also wondered how you felt seeing him after all this time?"

"It was weird especially since Micah was with me and it was just such a tragic situation anyway with both deaths. He spoke to me and gave me a hug."

"And?" her Mother said.

"And nothing, that was it. I received the flowers a little while ago and I just hung up thanking him."

"What is he up to Saniya?"

"I don't know Mama. He said he wanted to take me to dinner and talk."

"Have you talked to Micah about that?"

"No ma'am, I just hung up with Xavier and I wasn't sure what to do. I didn't give him an answer on dinner." Her Mama was silent for a moment as if she was choosing her words carefully.

"Saniya, I really like Micah and I think he is the man God has sent for you and I know that you really like him and care about him as well but I am still hesitant about you with Xavier. He is just too smooth talking and I question whether he really loves you but I know that he has told you that he does and I also know that he was your first. Things just get so complicated when you put sex in the equation, Saniya, and I think you and Xavier jumped into things too quickly. He already had experience in being a grown up and in being in relationships and by you giving up your virginity to him, he can train you and groom you to be the way he wants you to be in bed."

Saniya was blushing as her Mom was talking to her and feeling somewhat embarrassed.

"Saniya don't be embarrassed about all of this. If you are going to be grown, then be grown. There's a reason that we as women are supposed to wait and lose our virginity to our husbands. You are giving him a gift that no one else will ever receive and it is priceless."

"How old were you when you lost your virginity Mama?"

"I was 18 and it was to your Daddy Nosey Rosie and whether or not you ever realized it, I found out I was pregnant right before we got married. I was about two months pregnant with you."

"Mama, you had sex before you and Daddy got married."

"Yes, child and don't look so surprised. Your Daddy and I knew we were going to be married and we had already gotten engaged so we went all in. Now, I'm not telling you to do the same thing; even though that speech is a little late," she said smiling. "Although we are still married after all of these years. Neither one of us had a lot of experience in dating or in sex so we have learned together and that's what makes the journey fun Saniya, learning together. Now, it can also make it hard so that's why it's important to be in couple's ministry and ensure that you have good communication because marriage is hard work. There will be days that you are happy that you are married and there will be days that you think, why do I keep doing this or I would be better off single, but then you remember this man is your best friend and you remember how much you love one another. You need to pray about who you are supposed to be with Saniya. I am not going to brow beat you about Xavier because at the end of the day you are going to do what you think is best for you anyway."

"But how do I decide Mama? Micah is a great guy and I am having a blast with him. We have so much in common and Mama I love the fact that he has a good head on his shoulders and already has a plan for the next few years of his life both personal and professional."

"What are Xavier's plans for the rest of his life Saniya?"

"I really don't know. He has never really said."

"Trust me Saniya, I know you love, Xavier, but you can also grow to love Micah because I have seen the smile on your face when you are with Micah but again, you have to make that decision. We all have our own life experiences Saniya and your story will be different than mine. Don't lead Micah along if you are still in love with Xavier. It's not fair to him. Has the thought of sleeping with Micah crossed your mind?"

"No, Mama we are not going to sleep together. We have talked about waiting. He wants us to abstain from sex so that we can truly get to know one another."

"See, another reason why I like Micah so much, with his fine self." With that her Mom kissed her forehead and walked out of the room. After her Mama left and went downstairs, Saniya called Xavier and told him that she would go out with him for dinner. Xavier was excited and told her that he would pick her up tomorrow night at 7:00. Saniya was excited but apprehensive at the same time.

Later that day, Micah came to pick up Saniya and they decided to go riding and then head to the park and have a picnic before going shopping at the mall. Saniya was still trying to decide whether or not to tell Micah that she was going to go to dinner with Xavier. As they were walking through the mall, Micah asked her to wait while he ran to the restroom. Saniya sat down on one of the benches to wait for Micah and then she heard a familiar voice. When she turned around she saw Xavier talking and laughing with some girl and he had his hands all on her behind and she was staring up at him smiling in his face. Then he kissed her and as he turned around to grab the girl's hand and walk away, he saw Saniya.

As Saniya stormed over to Xavier and the girl, she yelled, "Really Xavier, Really? You are such a liar and a loser. You can cancel dinner for tomorrow night, I am done with you!!!" Saniya was so mad, she could feel her head getting hot, so she stormed away and went back to her seat to wait for Micah. The girl that Xavier was with looked puzzled as Xavier was trying to yell at Saniya and she kept walking away. About that time, Micah came out of the restroom and saw Xavier yelling out Saniya's name.

"Are you okay Saniya?" Micah could tell that Saniya was kind of frazzled.

"Man, I want you to stay away from Saniya, do you hear me?" Micah yelled at Xavier.

"I just need to talk to her man, just for a minute," Xavier said.

"Back off dude. I'm not going to say it again," Micah said in a loud authoritative voice.

Saniya was yelling at Micah. "Let's just go. I want him to leave me alone and stay away from me."

When they got in Micah's car, she told him everything that had happened even that Xavier had sent her flowers but she left off the detail about dinner. Micah hugged her and said Saniya, "I'm sorry that he hurt you and continues to plague you, but you know I will handle him if he keeps bothering you."

"No, no Micah I will make sure that he stops bothering me." Saniya then made her decision that she would be with Micah because nothing had changed with Xavier. He was still womanizing like always and she was not going to even consider getting back with him now.

By the time she got home, her phone was ringing. She looked at the phone and saw that it was Xavier and she let it go to voice mail. He continued calling non-stop even calling the house phone until she finally answered and yelled, "Xavier stop calling me, you liar!"

"Saniya, please listen to me."

"I am so done with listening to you Xavier. I want you to stay away from me and never contact me again!" Saniya could feel her eyes starting to water.

"To think, I was all set on having dinner with you and thinking about us getting back together again and then I see you today snuggled up with some other girl. I hate you

Xavier and I want you out of my life!" She slammed down the phone and lay across her bed crying.

Her mother wasn't sure what had taken place while Saniya had been gone but she could hear her daughter yelling and then crying from downstairs. She shook her head and then whispered, "Lord, please mend my daughter's heart and help her understand you know what's best for her." As Saniya lay in bed that night her phone buzzed and she picked it up and saw that it was Micah.

"Hello," she answered.

"Hey beautiful, I just wanted to check in on you and make sure that you were okay. I'm really sorry that I lost my temper today but I just got mad when I saw that he had upset you."

"No, Micah, I'm fine. I'm glad that you were with me and I'm glad that you were my knight in shining armor trying to protect me. I saw you in a different light as well today. I truly believe that you care about me and have my best interest at heart and I am thankful for that."

"Do you still need some time to deal with your emotions and all of this stuff with Xavier? If so, I would totally understand. Saniya, I realized today that I do have feelings for you and that I really want you to be my girl. I hope that you are feeling the same and that we can move forward and officially start dating."

There was a brief pause on the phone and she smiled, and he could tell she was smiling through the phone and she said, "Well, then it's official. I'm all yours."

ISLAND

Love on a Two-Way Street

Island was a bit nervous about meeting Taylor for dinner and he had no idea where the conversation would even start. It had been sometime since he and Taylor had sat down with one another and talked. The last time that happened was after she found out about his secret life and she was devastated. There were lots of tears and yelling and crying – it was a gut-wrenching experience for both of them. They had managed to talk on the phone a couple of times over the last couple of years once they had gotten their feelings out of the way and they had been civil with one another but they hadn't seen one another until now in Miami. To think, I will have to see this woman around here and around town for the next few months while we get this office up and running. I don't want it to be awkward, so we need to iron out some things now. Better late than never.

As Island sat waiting for Taylor, he thought about his escapade with Carlos last night. "Boy, what a night." Island thought about the fact that Chandra had not been part of what happened and he wondered if Carlos even told her that it happened. Normally Island felt bad the day after he had a fling but this time was different. "I'm not sure what is going on with me but I don't feel bad or feel guilty about what happened last night. I am tired of denying myself and trying to be someone else." Island was wrestling with himself over all of this.

"Like I was thinking earlier, maybe I should just have an arranged marriage like Carlos and Chandra and then I can still do what I enjoy doing but of course the issue is finding someone to go along with it. He really didn't think that Taylor would be willing to go that far with him regardless of how much she had loved him. He would love to give it another shot with Taylor and he could imagine himself being married to Taylor and having a beautiful life even with children. How would it all work? He wanted to talk to Carlos even more about this setup and how you find someone willing to do so. Not to mention, he didn't know that he wanted to go through all these hoops just for an image for work. He does want to become a vice president at his firm and was shooting for that position in the next few years.

"I just don't understand why we all have to fit in a particular mold for our society. People just don't value differences at all. It's already hard enough in this country for a black man and a gay/bisexual black man is even more of a challenge to people. My sexuality is my business and as long as I'm doing my job, then it shouldn't be a big deal even at the office. People are so judgmental in this society and some of the worst offenders are those that are in church." As

Island was reflecting upon his thoughts, he heard someone calling his name. It was Taylor.

"I'm sorry I was over here zoned out and didn't see you come in."

He got up and embraced Taylor. She smelled wonderful. He noticed how toned her body was when he embraced her and her curves were in all the right places in the black dress and pearls that she was wearing.

"Maybe, I'm not gay I just like both men and women." Taylor had certainly made him take notice and he did have feelings for her. He remembered that he thoroughly enjoyed being with her intimately, but she just didn't turn him on the way men did.

"Have you been waiting long?" Taylor asked.

"No, just a few minutes." As the hostess was taking them to their table, Island noticed that he was getting nervous and his palms were sweating.

"Wow, I haven't had this happen in a long time and why am I so nervous with Taylor now? I know that she isn't going to act a fool on me, we are past all of the emotions and drama. Well, I guess I will just wait and see what happens."

As they sat down at their table which was positioned where they could look out over the ocean Island thought to himself, "Well this is romantic."

Taylor started the conversation off. "Island, I must say that I was surprised when I ran into you the other day. I wasn't sure how I would react when I saw you again. Our last face to face didn't go over so well if you remember."

"Yes, I do, and Taylor I just want to say......"

"No, stop. Let me finish so that I can say all of this while I still have the nerve to do so. Island I want to say that I am sorry about how I acted when you told me about your secret life. I was so hurt and disappointed and I never saw that coming from you. You were the ideal boyfriend, lover and just my everything. It was like someone literally walked up and kicked me in the gut when you told me. I think after I finished cursing at you that I literally went into shock. I stayed in bed for days just crying and trying to figure out what I did wrong and what I could have done to make things better."

Island was feeling sick at his stomach as Taylor went over the rollercoaster of emotions that she experienced after he told her about his lifestyle.

"Then I started saying well maybe I'm not pretty enough or skinny enough. I actually started blaming myself for the decision that you had made. I was so upset that I couldn't tell anyone why we broke up. I ended up just telling people that we were just not made for each other and had decided to go our separate ways. I was too embarrassed to tell people that the man I loved was not into me but into other men. I wasn't sure how people would act or what they would say. To this day, my family and friends don't know what happened between us. They all just said we were the perfect couple and they didn't understand why we would break up. Finally, after months of me not saying anything about what happened they stopped asking and making comments. They could tell I was heartbroken and didn't want to make me feel even worse over the situation. It has taken me a couple of years and some counseling to finally figure out that our breakup wasn't my fault and if there was blame to be placed then it rested with you for not being up front and honest with me about your feelings. I really wish you had told me sooner Island before my heart became invested in you and all my emotions and my love. I have come to a point in my life where I can finally say "Island I forgive you." I forgive you for hurting me and cheating on me and most of all for not being honest with me about your life and what you were feeling. That's all for now."

"Taylor, I am so sorry that I put you through all of that and all of those various emotions. I really didn't know how to handle it all myself. I was trying to figure it out along the way. I hadn't even planned to tell you that night, but I just blurted it out before I knew it and I could see the shock on your face. My attraction to you and also to men is something that I have wrestled with for years. I am so sorry that I caused you a lot of pain but most of all I am sorry that I made you think any of this was your fault. It wasn't. My lifestyle and who I am had nothing to do with you but you were collateral damage while I was trying to figure out everything. If you would allow me, I want to tell you how all of this got started." Taylor shook her head yes and Island proceeded to tell about what had happened to him in high school and how he had kept it from everyone even his mother. He told her about how ashamed and embarrassed he was because another man had done this to him and then how it lead into the lifestyle choices that he has made in his life. As he began to share his story with

Taylor, he saw tears in her eyes and she told him how sorry she was that all of this had happened to him.

"Island, I didn't know and if I had known I wouldn't have said all of those horrible things to you that night."

"You didn't know and I know that you were acting out of hurt and anger. I only opened up this past year and shared what happened to me with my pastor, one of the deacons at our church and a Christian counselor and they have been helping me work through some things."

She hesitated. "Are you still..........?"

"Am I still interested in men? Yes, I am. I also know that I am also still attracted to you Taylor and I have noticed other women, so I don't think that I am homosexual but possibly bisexual."

Taylor wasn't sure what to say after he finished so she just listened and nodded her head.

"Taylor, I still think about you and dream about you but at the same time, I have this desire for men; they seem to be my preference. I would love to one day be married and have a family but I know that it will take a very special woman to deal with me. Needless to say, I am still working through all of this and I am not in any type of dating relationship until I figure out who I am and what I am supposed to be doing with my life. I know what the Bible says about what I'm doing but is it any different than someone who lies, or cheats or kills?"

Taylor shocked him and said, "No, it isn't. Sin is sin and God doesn't have a hierarchy for it. Once I got past my hurt and anger, I had to do a lot of soul searching myself Island

and I realized that I said some horrible things to you on that day and for that I apologize as well."

As they sat and talked the remainder of their dinner and drinks, Island remembered why he loved Taylor so much. She reminded him a lot of his mother. She had a sweet, kind, giving spirit and not only was she beautiful but also intelligent. She was everything that a guy could want for a wife, but the only thing he kept asking himself was, "Why isn't she enough for me?" He wanted to be with her, but at the same time, he wanted to be with Carlos and often thought of the time he was together with Carlos and Chandra. Was he some kind of sexual deviant or were there others like him who wanted the best of both worlds? He didn't share with Taylor that he had just been with Carlos last night. The night was going so perfect that he just didn't want to ruin it. As they were about to leave for the evening, Island walked Taylor to her car.

"I have thoroughly enjoyed hanging out with you tonight Taylor and I am thankful that you don't hate me and that you have also forgiven me for hurting you."

"Don't mention it. It was great talking and cutting up with you as well, Island. I have missed you and I forgot that we were great friends before we became lovers and got into a grown-up relationship."

"Yep, where did the time go? It seems like only yesterday that we were eyeing each other and then dating and now here we are a few years later meeting up again after a flurry of I love you, I'm sorry, I didn't mean to hurt you, etc."

As Taylor hugged Island, he lifted her chin, looked her in

the eyes and kissed her passionately. After the kiss neither of them said anything to each other, just goodnight.

Then Island, knocked on her window before she drove off and said, "Taylor, I'm sorry, I shouldn't have done that without asking you."

"Don't be sorry Island, I wanted you to kiss me and as you can see, I didn't stop you," she smiled and then she drove off.

Island realized that he still had feelings for Taylor as he could begin to feel his nature rise within for her and he believed that Taylor felt the same thing and he said to himself, "Where do we go from here, or better yet, what do I do now?"

LOLITA

Swept Away

Lolita's boutique business was booming and she was busier than she had been in a very long time. She ended up hiring a couple of more sales clerks and she was flying off to New York and Paris at least a couple of times a month to pick out new inventory. This year she was also planning to attend Fashion Week in New York, Paris, London, and Milan. She was still trying to figure out how to fit it all in her calendar. Each one of the Fashion Weeks in those cities were scheduled at various times. Fashion Week in New York and London were held in February and September. Fashion Week in Paris was held all four seasons; spring, summer, autumn and winter. So, she was going to have to schedule wisely to get all the fashion weeks on her calendar.

She couldn't believe how much her life had changed over the course of a year since she stepped out on faith and started her business. Her business was growing and doing great and she and Shelby had started talking more and more. Lolita was trying to stay close to her since she and James had decided to file for divorce. Even though Shelby had hurt her terribly, she couldn't let Shelby go through

159

her divorce all alone. She knew the pain of divorce and she wanted to be there for her sister regardless of what had happened between them. Plus, her niece and nephew needed family support during all of this. Lolita had prayed for Shelby, James, their children and even for Rashad. At the end of the day, they were all family and their lives were intermingled, in a dysfunctional kind of way, but for the sake of the children involved, all parties wanted to do the right thing and put aside their own feelings.

As Lolita sat down behind her desk to take a moment to herself, she was also in awe over her newfound love life. She had just picked up her voice mail messages and had a lovely message from Aiden. Lolita felt like a school girl whenever she was with Aiden. He was such a gentleman and he was going to accompany her to fashion week as well. This would be their first trip together. They had been getting to know each other over the last few months and things were going great. He was showering her with gifts and flowers and taking her to fancy restaurants. She didn't remember when she had so much fun. He treated her just like a queen wanting nothing in return. They had decided to take things slow and to make sure that they really got to know one another and that they had God in their relationship. They attended church service and social events together and he also went with her to bible study. They even had bible study together and discussed the scriptures. She had been in awe of this man especially when he covered her in prayer.

All the years of her being with Rashad they had not prayed together, studied together and he didn't pray over her so this was all new to Lolita and she was taking it all in. She enjoyed every moment with Aiden and her daughter adored him and he her. It was like the perfect blended family and she had finally introduced him to Rashad. Aiden had asked to meet Rashad. He said, "If I am going to be spending time with his child, then he needs to know that I am a decent man and that I only have your best interest and your daughter's best interest at heart."

Lolita was happy that things were going as well as they were but this is what happens when you let God lead and take the reins in your relationship. Aiden had even explained to Lolita that what she was expecting Rashad to do in their marriage didn't happen if he hadn't experienced that in his own home with his parents and the same for her. "We learn how to be married from watching our parents and grandparents. We often forget that when we become adults, we mimic what we see our parents do. If Rashad never saw his father pray over his mother or go to bible study with her then he would be prone to do the same thing. We forget that our parents are the ones that teach us how to be married and we mirror what we see. Many of them still don't talk to us about marriage and what is expected from one another." She was learning a lot from Aiden and she was enjoying it. He encouraged her in her business and in her personal life. He told her he would like to get married again and he understood now that he was older that he probably wouldn't have any more children. He had learned to live with that fact but in the meantime, he was going to spoil her daughter just like she was his own. They had also started going to counseling with Pastor Harris and Sister Harris because of the tragedies that they both had endured. They wanted to make sure that if they were moving forward toward marriage that they had gotten rid of all their emotional baggage from their past relationship. Lolita had to learn to love herself. She had realized that every man is not Rashad and that all men don't cheat and she couldn't hold Aiden under the same scrutiny that she did Rashad. Between her counseling sessions, couple's sessions and her growing relationship with God, her life was good. Lolita heard someone calling her name and realized it was Shelby.

"Hey there, how are you?"

"I'm good. I was just sitting in here thinking."

"Is everything with you and Aiden okay?"

"Yes, it's great. I was just thinking about how messy our lives were a year and a half ago looking back at where we are now. It is amazing how God can move in our lives if we just remove ourselves and our emotions and let Him handle things for us. He never said any of it was going to be easy or that our lives would be fair, but things just seem to flow so much better when we involve Him in every aspect." How are you doing with the divorce and how about the children?"

"Things are moving along. We have another 30 days before it will be final since we had to go through counseling for the children so it's all coming together. I didn't think it would be this hard, Lolita, but it is. I am really sorry for what I put you through."

"Hey, what's done is done and we can't take any of it back."

"I have also started counseling to see why I am the way that I am and why I didn't have a problem hurting you and James the way that I did. I think my selfishness is the result of our Mother leaving us." They both sat in silence for a moment reflecting on that day but not sharing with one another.

"Well, I wanted to talk to you about something and was going to call you and chat with you about it. Are you going to continue with your real estate career? I know that James made most of the money, but you were doing great as a Realtor, but is it enough for you to keep up your lifestyle?"

"I have a lot of decisions to make, Lolita, but right now I am fine financially. Even though James was upset with me, he has asked me if I want to stay in the house or if we should sell and split the proceeds. Either way, we will be fine, so money is not a big issue and I could learn to scale back anyway. Who needs 500 pairs of shoes anyway when your sister owns a boutique?" They both laughed.

"Well, I still want you to think about it. How would you like to come into the business with me here at the boutique? It is growing so fast that I am considering opening another location here in Nashville. I could always use someone to help out here or to go with me to Fashion Week and pick out items for the boutique."

"Oh my, that sounds wonderful Lolita. Can I get back to you once I'm through with my divorce and counseling, et cetera.?"

"Sure, you can, no problem. I have just hired a couple

of more sales clerks so I'm good for now. I definitely am considering expanding."

About that time, Lolita heard her assistant talking with someone in the store and then she came to Lolita's office.

"Ms. Lolita there's a lady here to see you. She said it was personal and wouldn't tell me anything."

Lolita and Shelby headed to the front of the store as her assistant lead them out of her office. When Lolita got to the front she could see the woman's back.

"Ma'am, may I help you?"

When she turned around she said hello Lolita and said hello to Shelby. Neither of them really recognized her but she favored Big Mama.

"Hello girls. It's me, your Mother."

Both Lolita and Shelby just stared at her for what seemed like hours, but it was only a moment.

Shelby spoke up first saying, "The only mother we have is dead. We buried her last week, so you can go back to that rock that you crawled out from under. She then turned around and stormed out of the store. Lolita was still standing in awe.

As soon as Shelby arrived home, she fixed herself a drink. She had enough excitement for a lifetime all in the last couple of weeks and months. Today was the shocker of them all when her Mother showed up at Lolita's store. About that time, she heard the doorbell and when she answered it was Rashad.

"Hey baby, how are you?"

"I'm okay, I guess." Rashad grabbed Shelby and gave her a kiss and a hug.

"What's wrong babe?"

"Well a little while ago, when I was at Lolita's store this woman showed up asking to speak with Lolita and wouldn't tell her assistant what she wanted so when Lolita went out to greet her I joined her. Well, it was our Mother. We haven't seen her since she left us with Big Mama years ago. We both just stood there with our mouths hung open. We didn't know whether to curse her out or hug her. I had all kinds of emotions come flooding over me and I just made a comment and stormed out. I don't know if Lolita talked to her or not but I just couldn't deal with that today so I just left."

"Wow, that is a lot to take in. I remember Lolita talking about how bad it was when she left you two. I'm sorry that she did that to you two and that she is now trying to pop back up in your lives." Rashad grabbed Shelby and hugged her, and he could feel the tension in her body, so he suggested a foot rub or back rub to relax her.

"It may make you feel better. Where are the kids?"

"Oh, they are gone with James for the weekend. He had something fun planned for them."

"So, what are you going to do since they are gone?"

"I really hadn't given it much thought because I'm so used to taking them to their events on the weekend. I don't know what to do with all of this free time."

"I tell you what, I'm going to spoil you this weekend. I will come back and pick you up in about 2 hours. Do you think that is enough time for you to pack? I am not taking no for an answer. I wouldn't dare leave you alone this weekend with the kids being gone; especially if you don't want to be alone."

"Okay that sounds like a plan." What are you up to Rashad?"

"You just be ready beautiful when I come back to pick you up."

Rashad was back at Shelby's house in the two hours like he said.

"Where are we going Rashad?"

"You just sit back and relax and take a nap and I will wake you when we arrive." So, Shelby did as she was instructed. When she woke up they were arriving at a beautiful bed and breakfast somewhere in the middle of nowhere. The bed and breakfast was on the lake in the woods and each room had its own balcony overlooking the lake with rocking chairs. When they arrived, there were two massage tables set up for them in the bedroom.

"You can go ahead and take a bath or shower. We will have our massages and then do dinner." Shelby agreed and went and took a long bubble bath. While she was soaking in the tub, Rashad brought her a glass of champagne. Once she finished, they both had massages and then got dressed for dinner.

"Where are we going for dinner?" Shelby asked.

"They have a private chef on staff here and he has prepared dinner for us tonight and I asked him to do your favorite." They had an appetizer, salad and then moved on to the main course which consisted of prime rib and shrimp. Shelby had forgotten how much Rashad knew about her.

"Well Mr. Rashad, you have outdone yourself."

"The best is yet to come. The chef has also prepared your favorite dessert – cheesecake. I have sampled it and it's the best cheesecake I have ever tasted."

"Oh my, I feel so special."

"You should feel special Shelby." The chef brought out her dessert. As Shelby was about to bite into her cheesecake, she noticed something shining in the decorative part of the cheesecake.

"What in the world?" Shelby asked. As she picked it up, she looked up and Rashad was on one knee.

"Shelby, I have been wanting to do this forever. Shelby, will you marry me? I don't want to spend another day without you and I know all of this has been messy but I have waited over twenty years to do this." He took the three-carat ring out of her hand and placed it on her finger. Shelby was in tears by this time.

"Well, what do you say Shelby?" She looked up and said, "Yes, I would love to marry you Rashad." About this time, the other people in the restaurant were all applauding them as they kissed. When they sat back down, Shelby said, "You got me good. I was not expecting all of this. I don't know if I can take any more surprises, but this has been the best one yet."

"You know that I talked with Sister Lula before she went home to be with the Lord and both her, and Big Mama told me that I should follow my heart. We both have hurt others along the way and we didn't mean to we just wanted to be together even though it was selfish the way we went about it. It seems like things are falling into place now that we have our emotions out of the way."

"Shelby, this is a chance for us to have a fresh new start. The start that we should have had years ago and didn't. I love you and I already love your children since they have been my niece and nephew all these years. They won't have to get to know anyone different but we will have to sit down and explain some things to them and hope that they understand. Shelby, I really want us to do this the right way so I have already scheduled some counseling sessions with Pastor and Sister Harris if that's okay with you. I know that your divorce is not final yet but once it is final, I want you to consider what kind of wedding you want and where."

As he gave her a glass of champagne, they toasted to new beginnings. "We will deal with everything else, one day at a time and that includes your mother. I don't want to rush so you set the date as to how long we will be engaged and when we want to get married. Just know that I have waited all these years, I will wait even longer just knowing that you are mine. Do you like your engagement ring?"

"I love it Rashad! It's absolutely beautiful. I don't think I have ever seen anything like it before."

"I hope not. I had it designed especially for you."

The rest of Shelby's weekend was amazing, and she was excited to be with Rashad. It was as if they never missed a beat. The just picked up where they left off years ago and continued their love story. In the back crevices of her mind, she still wondered if she was making the right move.

In the spiritual realm the enemy murmured to himself, "Now that all the excitement and hiding from everyone is over with, we will see how Shelby handles just being with Rashad. Will he be able to meet her standards and give her everything that she wants and needs? Will he be able to care for her financially and cater to her ways? Maybe, we need to see if Shelby really loves Rashad the way that she says she does."

DEACON JONES

A Companion of Fools

As Deacon Jones slowly made his way to the kitchen, he was startled by the lamp being on in the living room. As he looked up he saw Marcus sitting in his chair looking straight at him.

"Are you okay Daddy?"

"Yea, I'm fine."

"Well it didn't appear that you were fine. I had been calling you all morning and when I didn't get an answer, I came over and you were knocked out cold. From what I can see and how the car is parked, it appears that you were out drinking last night."

"Well, I uuuhhhhh."

"Daddy, are you serious? After what happened with Mama, you got behind the wheel of a car drunk? What in the world possessed you to do such a thing? Haven't we had enough hurt by your drinking?" Deacon Jones knew that he deserved every word of the hurt and anger that Marcus was throwing at him. He had beat himself up enough when he first woke up this morning.

"Daddy, I think you need to seek some professional help."

171

"I don't need any professional help. This is the first time that I have had a drink since your Mother's death. I felt so bad and so all alone after Lula and Imogene's death and I was feeling really down and out last night when Junior and JT called me wanting me to go hang out with them for a while."

"Where were those clowns when Mama died? Did they even come over here and see you? Did they come to the hospital or the funeral home? Daddy, just like you used to tell me, be careful who you call friend. Friends love at all times (*Proverbs 17:17*)."

"Marcus, I don't expect you to understand but I get so lonely here without your Mother and now my friends Lula and Imogene are gone as well. When you get my age, your friends' list gets short. I can't bother you and your sister all the time. You have your own lives to live and your own families to tend to."

"Daddy, you are our family as well. Do you think it would do you some good to stay with us every now and then?"

"I don't know. I have to think about it. I don't feel this way all the time, just right now."

"Well, Daddy, we don't want you feeling like you are all alone. We will do whatever we need to do to help you, but you have to let us know.

"I don't want you kids giving up your lives for me. I am more than able to get out and about. I just have to get back in the groove of things with my prayer group and back meeting with Pastor Harris and my counselor."

"Dad, you are still grieving. You are trying to rush the

process, but you must go through these emotions. I know men from your generation think that you have to be strong for everyone but you don't. It's okay for you to show that you are human and that you are not superman. We know you're not perfect and that you have vulnerable moments just like anyone else. We would be foolish to think otherwise. Now, I am still upset with you for driving home drunk. What if you had hit someone on the way home or ran off the road and injured or killed yourself? Daddy, you are all that we have left, and we want to keep you around for as long as possible. So, I am begging you not to do that again and stay away from your 'so called friends.' Did any of them even call to make sure that you made it home safely? I didn't think so."

"I got you son and thanks for being concerned. I promise this will not happen again. I was just having a pity party."

"Well you know what Pastor says about that – there's no one there but you and the devil. Daddy, don't you realize that you have made the enemy mad by changing your life around? I compare you to Paul/Saul, you were radically changed like Paul was and that has made the devil mad because he lost one of his best soldiers. You have now changed sides and are working for the Lord. The enemy is going to try and destroy you and everything that you love because of this. So, we all have to stay strong."

"Thanks son. I love you."

"I love you too Dad. Now, go ahead and call Pastor Harris."

Deacon Jones picked up the phone and called Pastor Harris.

"Hello?"

"Hello Pastor."

"Hey there Deacon. How are you?"

"I have seen better days."

"I have been wondering what you were up to Deacon. You have been on my heart a lot lately."

"Well, I had a relapse last night, Pastor, and I am just now getting out of bed. Marcus just chewed me out and lectured me. Now of course I feel horrible about what I did. Is it normal for people to backslide after being so on fire for the Lord?"

"Unfortunately, yes, Deacon. You are still human but the main thing you need to realize is that you need to repent and start again."

"I am having a hard time after losing Lula and Imogene. It just seems like all my friends are leaving here and there are some days that it seems like those around me just can't relate to me and what I deal with at my age."

"Deacon let's meet on tomorrow. We can talk and pray through some things. How is the prayer group doing?"

"Pastor, I'm afraid to say that we haven't been meeting over the last couple of months and it is evident by what happened to me. I just hope and pray that the other members are doing better than me. I plan on calling a meeting for next weekend if I can get everyone together. I know that Island is in Miami working for the next few months, so I'm not sure he will be able to make it, but you never know about him. He flies in and out of town every now and then. Saniya is dating a new guy."

"Yes. Micah. She introduced him to Sister Harris and I a few Sundays ago."

"I need to check in on Shelby and on Lolita. Once we meet, I will give you an update on everyone and whatever progress we have made or haven't made. Thanks, so much Pastor for being a listening ear to me with all of my drama."

"Deacon Jones, we are to encourage one another. Don't ever hesitate to call me when you are feeling down. I also want you to know that I don't have any magical powers. You can reach the throne room just like I can, but if you need a listening ear, then I'm here for you."

"Thanks. Have a nice night Pastor."

"You too, Deacon, and don't beat yourself up too much. What's done is done and tomorrow is a new day with new grace and mercy."

THE TRIBE

Back Together Again

As the tribe members began to arrive, Deacon Jones prepared the snacks for everyone.

"Come on in everyone. Make yourselves at home. You know where everything is after all this time. You all are no longer guests, but family."

They all came in and started helping Deacon put out the food. So far all the members of the tribe had made it. Saniya, Lolita, Shelby and even Island had made the meeting along with some new members. Deacon Jones opened with prayer and then shared with everyone that he had relapsed but he was now back on track again.

"I felt horrible about what happened. Here I am always trying to be strong for you all and encourage you that I was not paying attention to myself and what was going on inside of me. After speaking with Pastor Harris, he helped me understand that I am still grieving and that I have to go with the flow of things and not beat myself up when I slip up. I ask each one of you to pray for me. I am really lonely now with Lula not being around to talk to and hang out with. I will be hanging out with the Lord even more now. I realize that since everything happened with Lula that I had stopped reading my bible, stopped studying and we haven't met like we used to. We will get back on track for all out sakes. Anyone else want to share?"

Saniya shared that she was done with Xavier and had moved on and was now dating Micah. She didn't share that in her heart she was still in love with Xavier but was suppressing that because he couldn't remain faithful.

Lolita announced the big news that her boutique had opened and was doing very well. She also shared that she had started dating Aiden and everyone congratulated her. She shared that she had asked Shelby to join her in her business as well and told everyone that things were coming around between the two of them. Shelby announced that she and James were getting divorced and it was almost final. She apologized to Lolita in front of everyone and told that she realized how much she hurt her sister and that going through her own divorce helped her realize the damage she had done. She was not ready to share that she and Rashad had gotten engaged. She hadn't even told Lolita the news yet. She looked at Lolita and whispered our Mother and she nodded. Shelby also told about their mother showing up the other day and the mixed emotions that she and Lolita were dealing with.

Last, it came to Island and he just asked everyone to pray for him. "I am still struggling in some areas of my life and I need all your prayers while I am away. Like Deacon Jones I have backslid on some things and then my former girlfriend, Taylor is working on the same project as I am so I am having all these feelings surface about her as well. I need to be at these meetings even if you all have to Skype me in."

Afterwards, Deacon asked everyone to join hands and bow their heads so that he could pray. He reminded everyone that they are a work in progress. That some of these changes don't come overnight, and that this walk is a journey that will continue until Christ returns. He also reminded them that none of them are perfect but that they are forgiven.

In the spiritual realm, the enemy watched the group and listened, he had already decided who he would continue targeting. He laughed to himself because he knew a couple of them were easy targets but some of the others had started praying, studying and coming before God even more than ever. The Lord Almighty said, "*Remember, just like I told you with Job, you can do what you please, but you can't touch their souls. They belong to me.*"

"*Well we will see how much longer they belong to you once I finish with them.*"

"*Again, devil, don't you remember Job? Didn't you learn your lesson with him? Remember, my son died for all their sins and we win. You will be tossed back into the pit of hell where you belong one day real soon.*

As the group dismissed, they said their "goodbyes" and "I love you's" before going their separate ways. They all realized that Island and Deacon Jones needed a lot of prayer because they had been struggling but, in all consciousness, each one of them had areas that were struggles that they didn't share with one another.

In the spiritual realm, the enemy said, "Well I guess they don't trust each other as much as they think they do. Each one of them left out a tiny detail about what was going on in their lives. All I need is a crack to get in and by them not telling the entire truth, they left a crack in the door for me." He laughed to himself and said, "Now, who's next?

SANIYA

Now What?

Saniya heard the doorbell. She wasn't expecting Micah for another hour or so. She ran down the stairs and opened the door. She was in disbelief.

"Xavier, what are you doing here?" She hadn't seen Xavier in over a month or two. The last time she saw him was the blow up at the mall.

"As he pushed past her and into the house, he said, "Saniya, I just had to see you. I can't stand not being with you or being able to talk to you. I know I messed up again and I'm sorry. That girl didn't mean anything to me"

"Yes, you are sorry," Saniya snapped back. "I am with Micah now and I would really appreciate it if you would leave me alone!"

"I can't do that Saniya. All I do is think of you, baby please give me another chance."

As Saniya was turning around to throw him out the door, he slammed the door shut and pinned her up against the door and kissed her with all the passion that he had within him. Saniya could feel herself getting weak and wanted to resist his sweet luscious lips, but she couldn't. She tried to pull herself away but she was like a moth to a flame and could feel his body pressing against hers.

"Xavier, please......" He continued kissing her and moving down her body with his mouth and before Saniya knew it, Xavier was pleasing her in ways that she had forgotten that he could. She had not been intimate with Micah and her body craved the attention that Xavier was now giving her. He knew her body like a road map. He knew exactly what to do to take her ecstasy. She continued trying to resist but her body was burning with desire for Xavier and she surrendered herself to him and she forgot all about Micah.

ISLAND

Guess Who's Coming to Dinner?

As Island arrived at his Mother's house for dinner, he noticed that there were three place settings for dinner instead of two. Island knew that his Mother was having a hard time bouncing back after her two friends had died and he also knew that she was having some health issues. Deep down he thought that she was keeping her health a secret from him.

"Mama is someone else joining us for dinner?"

"Yes, we are having company for dinner, if that's okay with you?"

"Well, it's your house. Who am I to tell you whether or not you can have an extra person for dinner?"

"Before my guest arrives there's something that I want to talk to you about Island."

"Okay Mama, what is it?" Island could tell that his mother was extremely nervous, and she looked as if she had been crying.

"As I have been reflecting on my life this past year, I realized that I have not always been the best Mama. I have made some mistakes in life like everybody else."

"What you talking about Mama? You know you are perfect."

"No son, I'm afraid not, I'm far from it." As she cleared her throat she said, "You know you have always struggled with your father walking out leaving us and it has lead you down roads that I never thought about until now with your lifestyle choices. You don't hide things from me and now I am not going to hide anything from you." She cleared her throat some more and sipped on some water. "There's was more to your father leaving than I shared with you. You have to understand that your father and I didn't have a perfect marriage and that we had issues just like any other married couple. One night when your father was acting foolish, I had had enough, and I left the house. I went out on the town drinking and having myself a good ole time. I had a little too much to drink and I ended up ....and she paused for a moment. "I ended up sleeping with a man by the end of the night. I had never done anything like this before in my life and I just wanted to be held and loved by a man. It was a guy that I had met at the bar that night and I didn't even know his name and I don't know if he even knew mine. Both of us had way too much to drink."

Island's eyes had widened but he was trying not to say anything or make a face and let his Mama finish. Her eyes were full of tears by now and Island reached for his Mama's hand.

"Well Island the reason your father left us was because I became pregnant because of my one-night stand. There was a long moment of silence as Island began bracing himself for what his Mama was going to say next. "Your father is really not your father. Recently, I started remembering some things and I realized who your father was. It was like I had blocked out all of it until now. I have invited him over for dinner tonight so the two of you can meet and to let him know that he's your father. He will find out the truth tonight just like you."

There was a long moment of silence and Island didn't know what to say so he just sat down on the couch and was speechless. More like numb.

"Island, please say something."

"I don't know what to say Mama. I really don't."

"Son, please don't hate me but I can't take this to my grave and you both deserve to know the truth about one another."

About that time the doorbell rang and his Mama went to answer the door. Island could hear her talking and asking the man in and when they walked into the room. Island couldn't believe his eyes when he saw who his father was.

"Oh my God! Island exclaimed. The man's eyes widened, and he repeated the same thing.

LOLITA

The Second Time Around

As Lolita and Aiden bordered his jet, Lolita couldn't believe that she was now off to Paris on a private jet with Aiden. He had wined and dined her and romanced her and she now believed that she could love again. She had learned to love herself, but now she was learning to open her heart and love another man. Something she never thought possible again.

The flight attendant brought them two glasses of champagne. As Lolita raised her glass, she noticed something floating in her champagne flute.

"What in the world is this?" she exclaimed.

"What is it? Is something wrong with your champagne?"

"No but there's something floating in the bottom of my glass."

About that time, Aiden grabbed her glass and held it up and said, "Look carefully Lolita." As she looked at the glass, she could see a huge diamond ring in the flute.

"Oh my God is that a ......diamond ring?"

"Lolita, I never thought that I would be able to find love again and I never thought that I would even have a family again until I met you. You have been a ray of sunshine in my

187

life this past year and I love you. I have a question. Will you marry me?"

Lolita shrieked and scared herself. "Aiden, of course I will marry you!" she said with tears streaming down her face. She couldn't remember when she had felt such joy in her heart and she didn't want this moment to end. "Maybe fairytales do come true," she thought to herself.

SHELBY

Am I Overreacting?

"Rashad, I don't know why this wench continues calling Lolita and me. We don't want to hear her excuses and we don't need her in our lives right now."

"Honey, please calm down and we will talk about it later on tonight."

"I don't want to talk about her, I want to work on our wedding plans and forget all about her like she forgot about me and Lolita. "Where are you anyway Rashad? I thought you were on your way to my place by now."

"Babe, I'm finishing some stuff at the office and then I will be on by. I should be there by seven and then we can talk about the wedding and whatever you want."

"Okay, I miss you."

Before Shelby could finish saying I miss you and I love you, Rashad had already hung up the phone. Shelby and James had sold their beautiful home and split the proceeds. Shelby had rented a condominium until she and Rashad decided where they wanted to live.

Even though they weren't married yet, Rashad was having his mail forwarded to Shelby's address since she was budgeting their money. As she was going through their mail, she opened his bank statement and saw that he had spent an excessive amount of money on his last business trip. Shelby started reviewing the bill.

"Why is his bill so high? I thought he only stayed in New York overnight, but this bill is charging him for two days, what the hell is going on?"

Shelby's mind wandered back to the day that Lolita found out that she and Rashad were having an affair when she saw the same bracelet he had purchased for both of them. Shelby began to wonder if Rashad was really all in or what. She stopped her thoughts midstream.

"No, he wouldn't do that to me, he wouldn't."

As Rashad was driving home, he was thinking to himself and reminiscing. "Shelby will never know what hit her when I do this. She won't even see it coming," he smiled to himself.

DEACON JONES

Papa Was a Rolling Stone.

Deacon Jones was trying to figure out what to do next. For once he was at a loss for words and he was left speechless. He had to figure out how to handle this situation. Was there a way to protect his family from the truth? He was glad that Mona was not alive to see and hear all of this and what had taken place. He didn't know if he could handle any more news this year. He had taken on all the love, grief and hurt that he could take and now he had even more news that was going to turn his life upside down.

"Lord, what next?" I don't know that I can handle anything else in my life. I have caused my family enough pain over the last couple of years and now this because of my carelessness." The Deacon hadn't remembered anything until the story was being brought to his attention. It was still sketchy. He was only able to remember bits and pieces of what seemed like a dream to him but now he was finding out that his dream was not a dream but a reality. He knew that he didn't need to have a drink because that would spiral him out of control so he called on the name of the Lord so he would know how to deal with the news that he had just learned.

In the spiritual realm, "God, I told you that I would break them, and they would turn from you."

"No such thing has happened so don't get so excited. I know how much they love me and care for me and they will not turn from me. They will continue to trust me even in the darkest moments of their lives and even if they turn from me for a season, they will return to me just like the prodigal son. I promise you that. Remember, I am the Alpha and the Omega, the beginning, and the end. I must remind you again, WE WIN!"

DISCUSSION QUESTIONS

1. What are your thoughts on Saniya's new love interest Micah?

2. Why do you think Shelby is being insecure all of a sudden?

3. What growth did you see in each character if any from the first book?

4. Have you ever backslid as a Christian in your walk with God? If so, how did you get back on track? What did you do to get back on track?

5. Are you prone to forgive instantly or do you think that forgiveness is a process? What does the Bible say about forgiveness?

6. What do you see in our society that has become the "new norm" that we didn't see 10-20 years ago?

7. Do you think that fairytales set up young women for relationship failures?

8. Do you think that we use the word "Love" to loosely in our society?

9. Have you personally ever deal with the light-skinned or dark-skinned issue? If so, who was the

culprit or the person that made you take notice of the differences and the stereotypes?

10. Why is it so hard for the African American race to reach out and get professional help like counseling or therapy?

About the Author

Alicia Clemmons Fleming is a new up and coming author and *The Secrets between These Walls* is her first published work. Alicia lives in Mt. Juliet, Tennessee, a suburb outside of Nashville, with her husband David and dog Cody. When she is not writing, she loves reading, traveling and spending time with her family.

Made in the USA
Middletown, DE
12 October 2018